MY DOG
PAL

MY DOG
PAL

Storybook written by

Gail Hamilton

Based on the CBC TV series produced by
Sullivan Entertainment

WIND AT MY BACK

HarperCollins*Publishers*Ltd

MY DOG PAL
Storybook written by Gail Hamilton

http://www.harpercollins.com/canada
http://www.sullivan-ent.com/canada

First edition

Canadian Cataloguing in Publication Data

Hamilton, Gail
My dog pal

Based on the Sullivan Entertainment/CBC-TV series, Wind at my back.
ISBN 0-00-648159-0

I. Title.
PS8565.A5354M9 1997   jC813'.54   C97-930250-1
PZ7.H1816My 1997

97 98 99 ❖ WEB 10 9 8 7 6 5 4 3 2 1

Printed and bound in Canada

CHAPTER ONE

In the Bailey house, in the small northern town of New Bedford, the lights were being put out for the night. The house was large and grandly austere, reflecting the character of its owner, the elderly matriarch of the family, May Bailey. May had no use for "foolishness" of any sort, and she ruled with an iron hand.

Upstairs in the corner bedroom, May's grandsons were getting ready for bed. Hubert and Henry Bailey, known familiarly as Hub and Fat, were in their pajamas but not ready to sleep. Hub had forgotten to brush his teeth, so he made his

way down the hallway to the bathroom, closing
the bedroom door behind him.

Fat, who was ten, waited a moment and then
padded stealthily to the door. First he listened, and
then he creaked the door open just long enough to
allow a furry brown stowaway to slip inside. This
illicit third party was a dog named Pal. Pal belonged
to Mr. Murphy, the supervisor at the Baileys' silver
mine, and he was paying the boys to take care of his
dog while he was out of town.

As will happen when kids and dogs are put
together, both boys were already in love with Pal,
and Pal was in love with the boys. Hub and Fat were
certainly a great deal livelier and lots more fun than
Mr. Murphy, who left Pal shut up by himself in a
lonely yard day after day. As for Pal, he was exactly
the sort of dog any boy would adore. Of mostly
collie ancestry, he was a handsome fellow with a
long, inquiring nose, silky perked ears and a character that was mischievous through and through.

Pal immediately hopped up onto Fat's bed and
lay down, taking up most of the available space.

"Pal, you're hogging the whole bed. Move
over ..."

Fat had to whisper. If his grandmother ever
found out where Pal was sleeping, they'd both be
in a heap of trouble. Grandmother Bailey had a

long list of things she disapproved of, and dogs in boys' beds ranked somewhere near the top.

Pal gazed up at Fat but didn't move. Instead, he put his head down on his paws with a quizzical look. Fat got in and nudged Pal with his knee until Pal finally wiggled over, giving Fat room.

"Good dog," said the boy as he stroked the honey-brown fur of Pal's head. In response, Pal gave Fat a big, slurpy kiss that made him grin.

When the door creaked softly open again, Fat quickly hid the dog under the covers—but it was only Hub. Hub was twelve and wise to the ways of younger brothers. Fat smiled, trying his best to look casual, but he didn't fool Hub for one minute.

"Fat ... is Pal in bed with you again?"

"Shh!" whispered Fat in alarm. Grandmother Bailey was well known for her excellent hearing. Sheepishly, he peeled back the covers, revealing Pal—or half of him, at least. Pal's head popped up in a doggy grin, his tail wagging furiously and comically underneath the covers.

Hub shook his head, pushing aside a shock of brown hair from his forehead. "You know Grand-mother doesn't want him under the covers with you." Then, unable to help himself, he wagged a finger. "It's unsanitary, Henry," he squeaked in a parody of May Bailey's authoritative tone.

Fat smothered a guffaw and threw his arms around Pal's neck. "You're sanitary, aren't ya, Pal? Yeah!"

Pal put his head in Fat's lap and snuggled up. Hub shrugged, secretly pleased to have the dog in the room too. "It's your funeral if she catches you."

In the few weeks the boys had lived with their Grandmother Bailey since their father's funeral, they had more than once come nose to nose with her commanding ways. However, it was tough times, the Depression of the 1930s, and the boys had to stay put until their mother could find some way of supporting them.

Hub sat down on Fat's bed and patted Pal too. Pal rewarded him with enthusiastic licks. Fat regarded Pal with both pleasure and longing as he pulled his knees up under his chin.

"Hey, Hub ..."

"What?"

"You think we could ask Mr. Murphy to let us keep Pal when he comes back?"

This had been on the boys' minds almost since the first moment they had been given charge of the pet. However, Hub did not hold out much hope.

"I dunno. Even if he said yes, Grandmother would never agree to it."

May Bailey's house was full of expensive oriental rugs, brocade upholstered sofas and polished hardwood floors. Already she'd complained about the damage from Pal's paws and the hair from his long thick coat.

"I bet Mom would let us keep Pal. I wish things were the way they used to be," Fat said wistfully, remembering a different, happier life before it had all been blown apart by their father's sudden and totally unexpected death. "I wish you, me, Violet and Pal could live with Mom in North Bridge."

North Bridge, considerably bigger than New Bedford, was the town where Hub and Fat had grown up and where all their friends still were. Their father, Jack, and their mother, Honey, had run a hardware store for as long as the boys could remember. But hard times had been gripping the whole country for a long time. People couldn't buy as much as before—and when they really needed something, they often couldn't pay for it. Kind-hearted Jack had allowed his customers to run up bills, while he himself was running up a loan at the bank to keep going. One day the bank decided to call in that loan. Jack couldn't pay up so the bank seized the store and auctioned off every last thing the Bailey family owned—everything but the clothes on their backs.

Jack had had to swallow his pride and call his mother for help. May Bailey and her son had not spoken since Jack had married Honey, very much against his mother's wishes. But Jack had no choice. With no place to live, he had proposed that he move his family into a summer house on the lake—just until he could get a job and get back on his feet.

Hub would never forget their last day together as a family. They'd no sooner arrived at his grandmother's house than his father and grandmother had gotten into a terrible shouting match. Stomping out in a huff, Jack had piled the bewildered family into a rattletrap of a truck borrowed from the mine and roared up to the musty, rundown place.

But the family's stay at the lake had lasted less than an hour. Hub had been excited about the water and the sunshine and the idea of a fresh new beginning, and so had his dad. Together, they started to get the old canoe down to go fishing. All of a sudden, the canoe knocked down a hornets' nest. The hornets swarmed all over Jack and Hub, attacking furiously. But Jack was horribly allergic to stings. Hub held onto his father while Honey drove the old truck and they raced frantically for help. Despite the doctor's best efforts, Jack Bailey had died of his reaction to the stings.

After Jack Bailey's death, a grief-stricken and angry May Bailey had taken command at once— for May was very much a take-charge kind of person. The funeral was barely over when she insisted that two-year-old Violet, Hub and Fat's little sister, be given to a childless Bailey cousin to raise. And then she had declared that Hub and Fat would henceforth live with her. Their mother would have to look to her own relatives for charity.

Reeling from grief and totally broke, Honey had no choice but to leave the boys with their grandmother and go back to North Bridge to stay with her brother, Joe. But she'd made the boys a solemn promise: the moment she got a job and a place for them to stay, she would be back for her children—all of them—and May Bailey had better make no mistake about it.

The boys missed their father dreadfully, and being separated from their mother and sister only made things worse. But they found it was better to plan than to mope. So tonight, as they often did, they sat up in bed devising schemes, figuring out how they might get jobs of their own and help to get the family back together again. In fact, they'd already started—even though they would happily have done it for free, Mr. Murphy was paying them fifty cents a week to look after Pal while he was gone. It wasn't much, but every little bit helped.

They must have forgotten themselves and allowed their voices to rise, because the next thing they knew, the bedroom door had swung open, revealing the square, portly figure of their grand-mother. Hub scrambled to get into his own bed, even as Fat hastily dragged the covers back over Pal.

"Lights out, boys," May commanded. She stood very straight even though, at sixty-five, she now moved about with the help of a cane. Her gray hair was still thick and wavy though it was disciplined tightly into a bun. Her direct and pene-trating glance took courage to meet.

"Yes, Grandmother." Hub hunkered down, doing his best to look very sleepy.

May was about to leave when she noticed the peculiar lump in Fat's bed—a lump that seemed to be wagging at one end. Immediately she marched over, her cane tapping ominously on the floor.

"Henry, you've got that dog in bed with you again, haven't you!"

May refused to call the boys by their nick-names, which she considered undignified. She swept the quilt back to find Pal peering up at her sheepishly.

"Oh, for heaven's sake," May sputtered even as she pushed Pal sideways. "How many times do I have to tell you? You cannot sleep with this dog. It's not sanitary." She pulled Pal by the scruff of the neck right out of the warm bed. "Now don't let me catch you with Pal in bed again. Or there'll be trouble."

"Yes, Ma'am," mumbled Fat, who was really only sorry that he'd been caught.

May shut off the light and dragged Pal away. Pal barked at his captor, who scolded him as though he were just another naughty boy.

"Oh you hush. I'm going to put you out in the back yard where you belong, and that's final. Come along—out you go."

May ejected the reluctant dog from the room.

"Goodnight boys," she said over her shoulder.

"Goodnight Grandmother," Hub muttered in resignation. From Fat's bed came a pointed silence.

CHAPTER TWO

Pal did not spend all night sleeping by himself in the yard. Instead, he treated himself to a foraging

expedition in search of the perfect peace-offering
for the lady of the establishment. At sunrise, he
was to be seen trotting across the yard towards the
house, plumy tail held proudly high and the prize
of a dead crow in his mouth. Easily, he bounded
up the back steps, nosed his way through the
screen door and dashed into the house itself.

His toenails clattered lightly as he bounded
across the parquet floors, up the stairs and into
May's bedroom.There, he hopped up onto the bed
where May was sleeping and dropped the dead
crow smack on her chest.

May was so heavily asleep that she only stirred
a little. Taking this as an invitation, Pal crawled
right into bed beside her and rested his head on
her spotless, very sanitary, lace-edged white
pillow. The dog's weight plopping down caused
May to groan softly. Her eyes fluttered open just
enough to take in first a dog's furry face only
inches away, and then, on her chest, a stiff dead
bird.

The result was a bloodcurdling scream that rattled the lamps in the hall. Pal bolted crazily from
May's room, his feet scraping and slipping on the
polished wood floors as he scrambled along the
halls and ran down the stairs. In an instant, Grace,
May's grown-up daughter, appeared at the door of

her room in alarm, while Hub and Fat peered fearfully out from theirs down the hall.

"Bloody hell! Oh that blessed dog!" they heard May swearing.

Hub and Fat grinned and goggled at each other to hear their imposing grandmother give vent to a miner's oath.

Grace approached May's door tentatively.

"Mother, are you all right?"

The door was flung open, nearly knocking Grace over. May stood there, red-faced and furious. She was in her vast flannel nightgown and her hair was sticking out wildly around her head.

"No! Of course I'm not all right!"

She stormed towards the stairs, carrying the dead crow at arm's length, one of her fine linen hankies around its rigid yellow leg.

"If I ever get my hands on that wretched dog, I'll wring its blessed neck! If I don't burst a blood vessel in the process."

Pal, who had paused in the kitchen, now tore out of the house with May on his heels in hot pursuit. She so far forgot her dignity as to chase Pal all the way out into the back yard, with Hub, Fat and Grace right behind her.

"Get out of my house, you mutt! Get out of my house!" May was yelling at Pal as she brandished the dead crow above her head, as though she meant to pitch it after the dog as hard as she could. Instead, she flung one of the rubber boots from the pair standing on the back porch in case of rain.

Pal ducked it skillfully and vanished down the back lane at top speed. And who knew what shocking thing May might have screeched next had not Grace urgently shaken her elbow. Only then did May realize that just over the fence stood Mrs. Dorothy Grady, May's longtime neighbor, feeding the chickens she kept in a pen in her back yard. Mrs. Grady was staring with astonished and scandalized eyes at the spectacle May Bailey, the grande dame of all New Bedford, was making of herself. In an act of heroic self-control, May instantly composed herself and nodded a greeting, just as though she weren't standing out in broad daylight in her third-best nightgown, a dead crow dangling from her fingers.

"Good morning, Dorothy. Sorry about the commotion."

Mrs. Grady, a fussy, nervous sort of woman, was never at a loss for words.

"If you don't mind my saying so, May, I don't think you should let that dog roam through other people's yards."

Anything with teeth and an appetite was regarded as a threat to the Grady chickens. Mrs.

Grady especially disliked dogs. In Mrs. Grady's mind, dogs did nothing but scheme and plot about how to turn her fat fowls into doggy dinners.

"You needn't worry," May promised stiffly, casting a very meaningful look at the boys who had followed her out. "We'll be keeping him on a leash from now on."

Looking as though she'd believe it when she saw it, Mrs. Grady returned to scattering corn.

May's neighborly façade dropped away like a stone. Taking Hub and Fat by the shoulders, she pointed them back inside the house.

"As soon as you boys get dressed, I want you to go and find that dog and tie him up on the clothesline."

"But Pal doesn't like being tied up," Hub protested. And if Pal were tied up, how could he run free and play with the boys, as he had been doing ever since they had got him from Mr. Murphy.

"That's enough of your applesauce, Hubert. Now into the house you go, both of you." May pushed them on their way. "Go on."

As soon as they were dressed, Hub and Fat had no choice but to start scouting the back lane for Pal. The Bailey house, perched high on a hill, overlooked the town of New Bedford. From the lane, the boys could see the weathered wooden buildings of the silver mine in the distance—the mine that their grandfather had established.

Hub carried the dreaded leash as they both whistled and called.

"Here boy! Come here!" they shouted. "C'mere Pal!"

Partway down the lane, Pal appeared from behind a tree, barking at them joyfully. Pal was a dog who loved to bark—which was one more reason why May Bailey disapproved of him.

"Stay here, boy," Hub ordered, while Fat said, "Good dog."

The boys hurried over, but when Hub tried to hook the leash onto Pal's collar, Pal dodged them easily and loped off again. Several yards out of reach, he looked back and barked as if asking what they meant by trying to tie him up like that. Pal had had quite a lot of being tied up at Mr. Murphy's.

Fat set out after him. "Pal, come back here right now!"

Hub rocked back on his heels, knowing that Pal had no intention of giving up his freedom even for his two best human friends. "Forget it. We can chase him all day, he's not gonna let us put this leash on him."

"But Grandma said ..."

"Never mind what she said," muttered Hub, stuffing the leash into his pocket. "Do as I do, not as she says."

With this daring challenge, Hub turned around and walked nonchalantly away in the opposite direction. Fat trailed after him, glancing back over his shoulder at Pal. Pal woofed, ran a few steps and waited for them to follow as they had done before. Hub nudged Fat along when the younger boy showed signs of turning back towards the dog.

"It's not gonna work if you keep lookin' back."

They emerged from the lane onto the Main Street of New Bedford, a slow, sleepy thoroughfare that barely lived up to its name. Hub strolled past the few small stores with his hands in his pockets, keeping the leash out of sight. After a moment, Pal appeared around the corner of the fence, puzzled by the boys' apparent lack of interest.

Down the street, Hub covertly slid a small hand mirror from his jacket pocket and checked behind him. He could see Pal following them at a safe distance, his head cocked and his tongue lolling out.

"Is he still there?" Fat whispered.

"Yup."

Hub stepped over to a truck parked beside the curb.

"What are you doing?" Fat wanted to know.

"You'll see."

The truck was the local ice truck making a delivery. In those days, most homes had an ice box that kept food cool by means of a block of ice slipped into an insulated chamber so that it melted as slowly as possible, lasting until the iceman made the next delivery. Hub helped himself to a chunk of ice from the back of the ice truck. Dropping it on the sidewalk, he kicked it over to Fat.

"Keep passing it back and forth."

Fat kicked it back obediently, but without enthusiasm. His attention was on Pal, who was keeping cannily out of reach. He'd be darned if he could figure out what Hub was up to, but he followed his big brother's lead, as usual.

"Act like you're having fun at least, Fat."

Hub gestured for Fat to run ahead, then he kicked the ice chunk to him. The two boys began to dash along, passing the ice chunk back and forth, bodychecking each other, enjoying the roughhousing. The ruse worked. Pal, determined not to be left out of such a fun game, came racing over to them, barking as usual.

"Told ya," said Hub, just as Fat kicked the ice chunk far ahead.

"Go get it, Pal!"

Pal chased it, picked it up and ran back. After he dropped it on the ground, he jumped up and licked Fat's face, his ice-cold tongue making Fat giggle. Jumping down again, Pal raced ahead, barking for the boys to keep up the game. The boys continued down the street, kicking the ice, with Pal playing along, completely oblivious to the skullduggery behind it all.

Before Pal knew it, he found himself on the end of the leash and headed back towards the Bailey yard, where the boys at least had the grace to tie him to the clothesline so he could trot back and forth along its length.

Chapter Three

If Pal could have heard what May Bailey was saying about him, he might have hung his head in shame instead of romping cheerfully with the boys in the yard. It seemed that Pal had badly abused his privileges inside the house.

"Grace, that dog has chewed the arm off the

settee, chewed my patent leather shoes and scratched all the woodwork in the hall to ruin. And now, look at this, yesterday I found that animal standing on the dining room table playing with the wax fruit."

As evidence, May held up a twisted silver fruit basket held up by a bent silver cherub. The decorative fruit had clearly been gnawed at, and incriminating tooth marks dented the silver. "That dog is finished here," she declared furiously.

Grace was sitting at the table polishing some of the family's impressive array of silverware. At thirty, Grace was as slim as her mother was stout, and she had her hair set in the head-hugging waves so popular at the time. She had a face that was both pretty and kind. Her main problem was that she had been made unsure of herself by so many years of living as a dependent in the same house as such a strong-minded mother. If only she had married, maybe she could have escaped her mother's apron-strings ...

Now, at the sound of Hub and Fat laughing outside, she craned her neck to look out the window. Grace was pleased to see them looking happy again. With so many setbacks to cope with, they often seemed older and more serious than young boys have a right to be.

Following Grace's glance, May looked out the window too. Her features gathered into a scowl when she realized that the boys were playing with Pal.

Hub and Fat were hanging out with Buck, a lad of about their own age who was a new friend from the neighborhood. Oblivious to the storm gathering indoors, the three were doing their best to turn Pal's clothesline captivity into a lark. Ingeniously, they had rigged the wicker laundry basket into a gondola and sent it racketing from one end of the line to the other, with Pal aboard for the ride. Buck and Fat ran the dog back up to Hub, then sent him down again. Pal went sportingly along with this game, his tongue lolling out in pleasure and his feet braced against the edges of the swaying, precarious conveyance.

"Okay Pal, stay there," Hub encouraged. "Good boy. Now Fat, push him back. Come on, faster."

At that moment, May sailed out of the house, with the day's mail in hand, and was nearly struck by her own laundry basket whizzing by.

"What the devil is going on out here?" she demanded.

Hub scrambled for an answer. "You told us to put Pal on the clothesline, so we did ..."

"That's not what I meant, young man, and you know it. Now tie that dog up properly as I told you, and no more monkey business."

Suddenly Pal leaped from the laundry basket, jumped up on May and playfully grabbed the letters right out of her hand.

"Oh no," groaned Fat. Swiftly, he grabbed the mail from Pal and handed it back to his grandmother.

"Oh good grief. Tie that dog up. By Jove, if he chews one more piece of anything, I'm going to have him sent away."

With distaste, May wiped off a telegram and tore it open. If May was annoyed before, she became doubly irritated when she finally read its message. "Well, he's got a nerve!" she exploded.

"Who's got nerve?" asked Fat, shaking his brown hair from his eyes.

"Mr. George Murphy, that's who. He's been detained on his holiday by family business. He isn't going to collect that animal of his for another two weeks."

The boys almost broke into cheers but caught themselves just in time. May shot Hub a glance and discovered him grinning from ear to ear.

"Wipe that grin right off your face, Hubert Bailey. Don't you boys think for one minute you're leaving me alone with that holy terror of a dog to tend to when you start school tomorrow. He's your responsibility." She turned on her heel and headed inside. "I'm going to telephone cousin Meredith and have her come and collect that animal. She can take it out and keep it on the farm for the next two weeks."

Hub was instantly crestfallen. "But ..."

"But nothing! That's the end of it," his grandmother snapped over her shoulder. "I've had dogs in this house for thirty odd years, and never a moment's trouble—but this wretched animal is like a spoiled child!"

Since Pal hadn't been raised by May from a pup, he was totally ignorant of all the many rules and prohibitions that had kept all the Bailey dogs in line. Mr. Murphy hadn't bothered applying any rules at all, which was why Pal was a blissfully rambunctious creature without a scrap of etiquette to his name.

When May had gone inside and shut the door firmly behind her, Buck strolled over, his face full of sympathy. He nodded lugubriously towards the dog.

"I guess you guys can kiss old Pal goodbye. If he's going to the farm, he's a goner."

"What're you yapping about?" rumbled Hub.

"My Pa sent my dog, Boomer, to the farm and he never came back."

"So?"

Buck realized the pitiful depths of their ignorance. He lowered his voice ominously. "So don't you know what it means when they say a dog's going to the farm?"

"No ..." Fat began to look uneasy. "What does it mean?"

Buck jerked his finger across his throat and made a horrible sound to illustrate. Hub's and Fat's mouths fell open in horror simultaneously as they finally got the message. Going to the farm was the New Bedford way of saying that May meant to have Pal disposed of permanently!

The boys just had to help Pal avoid this awful fate, at all costs. If they couldn't keep him, they'd have to find someone else who could.

Hub and Fat turned to their one real friend in New Bedford, Max Sutton. Max was a schoolteacher, in charge of the athletics program. Shortly after their father's funeral, when the boys had run away to live at the summer house on the lake, it was Max who had discovered them there, and Max who had saved them when Hub had cut his leg with an ax and Fat had nearly burned the house down trying to help him. He had taken a real interest in the boys, and had even managed to coax Hub into playing basketball at the Boys' Athletic Club. Now, Hub regarded him as someone he could turn to in a pinch.

The boys found Max busy repairing a beaten-up old motorcycle in the driveway outside the house where he rented a tiny apartment. In a rush, Hub and Fat explained their problem while Max fiddled with the carburetor.

"Umm, listen fellas," Max began, "I'd love to help you out ... but I'm sorry, I can't keep a dog in my little apartment up there."

"Please, Mr. Sutton," Hub begged, "could you just let Pal stay here in the yard? We only need a place to keep him until Mr. Murphy gets back from his vacation in two weeks."

Fat was even more desperate. "Otherwise Grandmother says he's goin' to the farm—and you know what *that* means." Apparently Max wasn't familiar with this New Bedford expression either, so Fat repeated Buck's gruesome gesture to illustrate the point.

How could Max hold out against such a plea? Before he knew it, Max found himself over at the Bailey house watching Pal being untied.

May stood nearby, her hands on her hips. She

wasn't sure why the boys didn't want the dog sent to cousin Meredith, but she was very pleased to be getting rid of Pal in any case.

"Well, I never thought I'd see the day when I'd be thanking you, Max Sutton," May told him, "but it saves me the trouble of sending him to the farm."

Hub gave Max an I-told-you-so look about the terrible end from which Max was saving Pal.

"Not a problem, Mrs. Bailey," Max assured May, even though he looked pretty doubtful about this brave statement. "When the boys explained the situation I was glad to help."

"Come on, boy," Hub urged a reluctant Pal as he handed Max the leash.

"Well, you have more heart than brains," May informed Max, with a tilt of her chin.

Since this was not the most flattering thing to say to a schoolteacher, Max only nodded and began to drag Pal away. Pal did not know Max Sutton and could not understand why he was being parted from the boys he adored.

May turned to her grandsons, who were, after all, the ones who were supposed to be looking after the dog.

"Now you boys are going to have to share the money you got from Mr. Murphy with Mr. Sutton. It's only fair."

"Yes, Ma'am," Hub agreed, brightening up at once.

"Goodbye Mrs. Bailey, boys," Max called out as he and Pal set out. "Let's go, Pal."

They all watched Max and Pal cross the wide grassy lawn and vanish past a clump of lilac bushes. Pal went with his tail down and many bewildered looks back at the Baileys.

"Well, now we'll get some peace and quiet without that blessed dog tearing up the place," May declared, and she headed inside, intent on cleaning every trace of Pal from her fine home.

CHAPTER FOUR

May spent the afternoon sweeping up dog hair, but she could not sweep Pal from the minds of two lonely boys. All the rest of the day they thought about their faithful friend, tied up and with no one to play with him.

That night, at bedtime, Hub sat cross-legged on his bed reading a boy's adventure book. Hub had always loved to read, and since moving to New Bedford, he had taken refuge more than ever in books.

Fat, clad in his striped pajamas, slipped a balled-up dinner napkin out of the pocket of the pants he had been wearing all day. He unrolled the napkin to reveal a bone and some rather juicy meat scraps.

"What are you doing?" Hub asked, noticing out of the corner of his eye.

"I saved some scraps for Pal, from dinner."

"That stuff'll go rotten before you get a chance to see him again."

"We could see Pal tomorrow," Fat suggested hopefully. Max Sutton did not live far away, and surely Pal wouldn't mind how old the meat scraps were.

Hub shook his head. Now that their father was dead, Hub had begun to feel more responsibility for his younger brother. It would be better for him to face the hard reality right away. He mentioned the truth that he himself didn't want to think about.

"You're only making it harder on yourself, Fat. Mr. Murphy is coming back to get Pal anyway in two weeks, so we might as well get used to the fact that we're not gonna see him anymore."

Fat rolled the food into the napkin again. Then he couldn't help venturing the idea they had been mulling over the night before. "What about going to Mr. Murphy to ask him to let us keep Pal?"

Hub let out a sigh, suddenly feeling so much older than Fat. He too wanted, with all his heart, to keep Pal. In a town where Hub was a lonesome stranger, the dog had instantly become a loyal and unquestioning friend. Hub had only to romp with Pal for a few minutes to forget all the hardships he was trying so hard to get over.

"That was just wishful thinking, Fat. You know Grandmother would never let him stay here now. Pal's gone for good, and there's nothing we can do about it."

Fat slumped down on his bed, dejected. Even he had to admit that what Hub had said was only too true. He wished he could hug Pal right now and feel Pal happily licking his face. Yet when he looked over to Hub for a shred of hope, Hub just kept on reading. Fat didn't know that this time the book was hiding Hub's real feelings. Hub was having a hard time keeping up his tough guy act, but he was trying, for his brother's sake.

Pal certainly must have missed the boys as much as they missed him. Later that night, an energetic shape with a feathery tail appeared in the lane behind the Bailey house. Max Sutton, when he had shut Pal into the yard for the night, hadn't understood that the dog was an accomplished escape artist. Once darkness fell, Pal made short work of finding a loose board and squeezing through the fence, intent only on speeding back to the boys he yearned to be with.

However, just as he seemed ready to lope up to the Bailey house, he suddenly swung around, sniffing the air. His tail shot up and his nose went to the ground. A hotly tantalizing scent caused him to veer into utterly forbidden territory—the Grady backyard. In fact, the trail led him straight to the Grady chicken coop, where he ranged up and down along the wire mesh. The chickens, who ought to have been peacefully sleeping, were restless and active, already upset about something.

Suddenly, Pal spotted the trouble. A fox had gotten in amongst the chickens and was silently stalking a plump hen. Terrified, the chickens were now flying in all directions and squawking at the top of their lungs. Wildly excited, Pal began barking and racing round and round the outside of the coop. Then he began to dig madly at the wire, trying to get at the fox inside.

The uproar brought Hub and Fat sitting bolt upright in their beds.

"That sounds like Pal," exclaimed Fat. "He musta missed us and came back."

Racing to the window, they peered into the darkness. All they could hear was a frustrated yowl from Pal, who couldn't get at the fox, and the panicked cackling of the chickens. Hub had never heard Pal sound that way before.

"Hey, something's wrong. I'm gonna see what it is." Hurriedly, Hub pulled on his slippers and opened the window to slip out.

"Me too," Fat said, getting ready to follow.

"No, you stay here." Hub wasn't sure what was out there and he didn't want Fat tagging along.

"Why?"

"Because you'll fall and break your neck! Look!" Hub pointed out the window at the two-storey drop. The only escape route was a flimsy garden trellis that ran up the wall.

Fat was about to argue, but looking out the window, he thought better of it.

"Okay, at least give these scraps to Pal for me," he asked, holding out the napkin he had saved from dinner.

Hub grabbed the napkin, tucked it into the pocket of his bathrobe and climbed out the window. With some difficulty, he shinnied down the trellis in his pajamas and slippers, which did not grip the weathered wood very well. He finally dropped to the ground and padded out to the edge of the yard, keeping out of sight behind a tree. Carefully, he whistled for Pal.

Pal was now inside the chicken coop. He was racing around after the fox, and he almost had him, but just an inch away from Pal's teeth, the fox made its escape under the wire and streaked past the Grady house. Pal scrambled out in hot pursuit. In fact, he was about to intercept the would-be chicken thief when his ears perked up. He had caught Hub's whistle and skidded to a halt. Badly torn between his desire to chase the bandit and his desire to please the boy he loved, Pal hesitated. When Hub whistled a second time, loyalty won out. With a last, sad glance after his fleeing quarry, the ever-faithful Pal quickly changed direction and ran to Hub.

Hub had been about to give up when Pal loped up, grinning his doggy grin and ready to jump all over Hub in delight.

"Hey, Pal!" Hub whispered as Pal licked his face in jubilant greeting. "Hey, I got something for you ... shhh."

Hub unrolled the napkin and watched while Pal happily gulped down the tidbits that rolled out. He was not expecting to see anyone else in the yard after dark, so when he heard the back door creak, Hub ducked behind a thick chestnut tree and peered cautiously around to see who had come out.

"Grace! Grace Bailey!" he heard his grandmother call from her bedroom window.

"Yes, Mother?" came Grace's voice.

"What are you doing outside? That Judd Wainwright just telephoned to bother us again."

Judd Wainwright was a fellow who had admired Grace since high school. Grace had been very taken with Judd, too, but had been unable to outface her mother's disapproval of this "unworthy" suitor. They hadn't seen each other for years, and then Grace met Judd again on the bus to North Bridge, and he had offered her some much needed attention and support at a difficult time. Judd's interest in Grace had immediately revived, much to Grace's surprise and bewildered pleasure. The fact that Judd was now a large, loud, traveling pharmaceutical salesman did not bother Grace. However, Judd was no closer to being the sort of suitor May was likely to approve of for her only daughter.

"Sorry, Mother. Ummm, I forgot my purse in the car."

Even to Hub's ears, Grace sounded distinctly evasive. Soon, Hub saw why. Grace, in her coat and slippers, sneaked around the side of the house and fumbled to light a cigarette. If there was anything guaranteed to send May Bailey into apoplexy, it was the sight of one of her family puffing on the "evil weed."

Grace was not a practiced smoker. She managed to get the cigarette lit, inhale a little and then had to smother a barrage of coughs. When she had recovered she began, to Hub's astonishment, to wave the cigarette theatrically, the lit end making thin orange arcs in the dusk.

"The men I know ... oh, they're so polished, so nice, so considerate," she crooned in a sultry voice—apparently to the empty air in front of her. "Most women like that type."

While Hub stared, Grace leaned back, a hand on her hip, her head tilted at what could only be described as a rakish angle. "I guess they're afraid of the other kind," she continued, this time a little louder. "I thought I was too."

She broke off to take a pretend puff from the burning cigarette dangling so gingerly from her fingers. Then she edged closer to some imaginary listener, one shoulder dropping vampishly.

Hub crouched behind the tree, hardly able to

believe his eyes. In fact, he was seriously wondering whether his Aunt Grace might be losing her marbles.

Pal cocked one puzzled ear at Grace, then the other. A moment later, he left Hub and trotted towards Grace as if determined to find out what was going on. Grace had her back turned and was actually fluttering her eyelashes at the eaves trough. "But you're strong," Grace crooned, gazing up at the porch pillar adoringly. "You don't give, you take. Oh Tommy, I could love you to death!"

"Pal, no ..." Hub whispered urgently when he realized where the dog was heading.

Pal barked anyway, so startling Grace that she dropped her cigarette. When she recovered, she quickly tried to wave the dog away while at the same time scrambling to retrieve the lighted butt before it set the porch on fire. Pal, thinking it was a game, frisked about and yipped even louder.

Above their heads, May slid her second-floor bedroom window open, causing Grace to glance up in panic.

"Grace! Why are you taking so long?"

"Oh geez ..." Grace muttered under her breath. Frantically, she ground out the cigarette under the heel of her slipper, hoping that the telltale stink of

cigarette smoke was not wafting all the way up to
the upper storey.

"Grace? Grace, are you there?" May called
again.

Grace gave up and stepped into view. "Yes,
Mother," she answered resignedly. Pal barked
and trotted up to sit down loyally beside her.
May caught sight of him instantly and leaned
out.

"What's that blessed dog doing back here
again?"

Grace latched onto Pal as an excuse for lingering. "I don't know. I, um ... found him digging in
the garden and ... so I stopped to chase him off."

"Well, hurry up and do it then. But I want you
to come and telephone that Judd Wainwright
before he bothers us again." The less they heard
from Judd the better, as far as May was concerned.

"Yes, Mother."

May finally ducked her head back in and
slammed the window shut.

Expelling a sigh of relief, Grace grabbed Pal by
the collar and hauled him across the lawn. "Go
home before you get me into any more trouble,"
she muttered.

Pal broke away from Grace at the edge of the
lawn and sped straight back over to Hub, who was

still pressed up against the tree. Grace saw the pale flash of his pajamas before he could get out of sight.

"Hubert ... what are you doing outside?"

"'Ah ... I was just giving Pal some bits of food, from dinner."

Grace shook her head ruefully. "If your grand-mother catches you out here she'll have your head for sure ... or mine ...!"

"I won't tell anyone if you won't." When Grace looked puzzled, Hub lowered his voice and ges-tured towards the porch. "About the you-know-what ..."

When Grace looked even more puzzled, Hub mimed smoking a cigarette, and embarrassment flooded into her face.

"Oh dear, I wasn't really smoking. I just," she grew even more rattled, "I mean ... I think it looks so sophisticated in the movies that I like to play ..." Hub looked so confused that Grace gave up trying to explain grown-up fantasies. "I was only fooling around," she told him, with what she hoped was a nonchalant shrug.

In fact, Grace had been acting out a piece of movie dialogue. This time, she had been mimick-ing Jean Harlow in the film *The Public Enemy*. Pretending to be a bold and daring woman from the pictures was one way Grace could escape, at least for a few moments, from being forever at her mother's beck and call.

"As I said, I won't tell anyone if you won't," Hub assured her, beginning to feel a bit of a friendly co-conspirator with his aunt.

Grace glanced reflexively up at May's window and bit her lip.

"Well, I shouldn't encourage you, but I, I don't suppose any harm is done if you promise you'll never do this again."

"I promise."

"That's good." Grace relaxed. "Well, I guess I've gotta take Pal now." Grace tried to tug Pal by his collar but he resisted, looking up at Hub.

"Bye, Pal," Hub told him slowly. "I'll see you later."

Pal took the hint and reluctantly allowed Grace to escort him.

Before Grace was out of sight, Hub called after her, "You know, I smoked a cigarette once. It made me puke."

"Oh dear," laughed Grace, "I certainly don't want *that* to happen. I'll be sure to quit first thing in the morning."

Smiling to himself, Hub slipped back into the house before his grandmother caught him lingering outside, too.

CHAPTER FIVE

The next morning the boys were routed out of bed
extra early. It wasn't just any old morning, it was
the first day of school in New Bedford. Hub and
Fat would have to face an entirely brand new
beginning, and May was making sure they were
turned out smartly enough to do the Baileys
proud.

To this end, she sat Hub in one of the kitchen
chairs with a towel around his neck while she
trimmed his hair. Hub longed to squirm but didn't
dare. His grandmother was already dangerous
enough with scissors in her hand.

"Don't take too much off the back or
everyone'll tease me."

All Hub's friends were back in North Bridge.
Now, like any newcomer, Hub wondered anxiously about how he was going to fit in with a
whole school full of kids he didn't know. May
merely took another great whack at his bangs.

"Oh you needn't worry about anyone calling
you names. You just remember, you're a Bailey.
That means a great deal around here. For heaven's

sake, the New Bedford school was founded by your grandfather." May whipped the towel from around Hub's neck and stood back to view her work critically. "There, you're finished. Call your brother, he's next. And Hubert, always remember to wash your hands and feet and change your socks. Otherwise you'll smell like an old cheese." If this was May's idea of equipping her grandsons for the trials ahead, she'd totally forgotten what it was like to start at a new school.

As Hub slipped out of the chair, he winked at Grace, who stood at the counter making sandwiches for the school lunches. Flushing a little, Grace winked back. When Hub disappeared down the hall to finish getting ready, Grace watched him go, a small smile creeping over her face. The more Grace got to know her nephew, the more she liked him.

"Mother," Grace suggested suddenly, "are you sure you don't want me to take the boys to school? It's their first day ... and they really don't know anyone."

May shook her jowls at the suggestion of such coddling. "How am I going to teach those boys to be independent and self-sufficient if you keep babying them all the time?"

"I'm sorry, Mother. I just thought ..."

"Well, you shouldn't think so much, Grace. It's better if they do something on their own without us hovering over them like mother hens. It builds character."

Grace, who longed passionately to be able to do things on her own, could be forgiven for wondering why such training in independence had not been exercised upon herself in her growing-up days. She kept further comments to herself as Hub and Fat set out on foot, carrying their lunch bags and looking fearfully spruced up and scrubbed.

The boys had clean shirts, short vests with diamond patterns on them, wool pants that prickled against their skin. The freedom of summer seemed miles away. Hub ran his fingers through his hair, completely messing up the way May had combed it neatly back with water. He was not happy about his grandmother's handiwork.

"Ah, I wish she hadn't taken so much off. I look like some goody-goody choirboy."

They marched on in silence through the streets until they found themselves in front of Max Sutton's apartment. Pal, who had been sleeping off his night's adventures in Max's yard, woke up at their familiar step and jumped joyfully to his feet. In a moment, he'd popped the gate to the yard open and raced out to meet his favorite people in the world.

"Hiya, Pal!" Fat lighted up with pleasure. He ruffled Pal's ears vigorously, then dug deep into his pocket. Pal poked his nose against Fat with lively interest.

"Want something, Pal?"

Fat produced a strip of roast beef saved up from last night's dinner. It was now dried up and gray, but Pal gobbled it down with relish.

Hub made a face, teasing his brother. "Oh, I can't believe you're carrying that piece of meat with you. No wonder you smell so disgusting."

Ignoring Hub, Fat continued to roughhouse with Pal, letting the dog lick his face enthusiastically. Pal was getting dusty paw prints all over his trousers and snuffled at his pocket in case there should be some more tasty dinner scraps in there, but Fat didn't care.

"That's it," spluttered Hub in mock horror, marching away from them. "I'm leaving before people start thinking we're related."

Fat stuck his tongue out at his brother's back, continuing to ruffle Pal's ears. "You wanna go to school with us, Pal?" Fat asked the dog.

Pal woofed happily and trotted along beside Fat, ready to go to the opera or a square dance if need be, so long as he could be with his boys.

Hub, glancing back and seeing Fat and Pal gamboling along together, stopped in exasperation.

"We are *not* taking that dog to school with us!"

His words didn't have the least effect on Pal, who was jogging in circles around Fat, the morning sunshine making his rich amber coat glow. Shaking his head, Hub turned and marched on ahead.

By the time the little trio arrived at the school, the bell was already ringing and New Bedford children were hurrying inside into the halls.

The school, like everything else the Baileys had founded, was substantial and solid. It was built of dark brick with wide steps leading up to wooden doors. By the time Fat arrived, Hub had already gone inside. Unfortunately, Pal had to stop on the school steps. Even Fat did not have the nerve to let a dog inside the school.

"It's the end of the line, Pal," Fat told him dolefully. "You can't come in. I'll see you after school, okay?"

When Fat disappeared inside, leaving Pal all alone, Pal dashed up to the closed door and whined in bewilderment. He'd just met his beloved boys again and already they had left him all alone.

When he found no one would open the door for him, Pal ran down the steps and around the side of the building. He wasn't going to be parted again from Hub and Fat if he could help it, and he was looking forward to a day of fun and games.

Inside, Hub found his class and took a seat near the window, looking out over the schoolyard. Max Sutton, now dressed in a suit and looking very official, stood at the head of the room in front of a heavy wooden desk. A map of the world hung at one side of the room, the vast British Commonwealth showing up in red, and a shelf containing a set of well-thumbed encyclopedias graced the wall opposite Hub. When the students had all settled down, Max went to the blackboard, picked up a brand new piece of chalk and wrote his name in large, firm letters.

"Good morning, class," Max began, turning back to the room. "My name is Mr. Sutton. And, as some of you may already know, I'll be teaching the boys' phys-ed classes and I'll also be concentrating on Social Studies and Geography. I'm going to be your home room teacher this year, so I'd like to take this opportunity to welcome you all to my class."

Max had just opened his mouth to issue further instructions when there was a scrabble of claws at the window. Pal had spotted Hub inside and was trying to get into the schoolroom himself. When he couldn't, he began to jump up and down, barking rapidly to get Hub's attention.

"Hey Hub," chuckled a redheaded boy behind him, "did ya have to bring your dog to school?"

A wave of titters swept the classroom, causing Hub to turn quite red. The very last thing a new boy needs is to be singled out as an object of fun. Hub tried to wave Pal away with a few sharp gestures, but to no avail. Pal only thought Hub had finally noticed him, so he pressed his damp nose against the glass all the more eagerly, making smears. Helplessly, Hub looked at Max, who was equally chagrined by Pal's appearance. After all, Max was the one who was officially looking after the miscreant, and the last thing he needed was a breakdown of discipline on the first day of school.

"Uh, Hubert ... maybe you'd like to open that window and send that dog away."

More snickers traveled up and down the rows. Everyone stared at Hub, who now felt a flush of embarrassment moving down his neck.

"Yes, sir." Hub had to go to the window, heave it up and stick his head out. "Go home, Pal," Hub ordered rather desperately, pointing for Pal to go.

To Pal, this was only a signal to try to lick Hub's face. When he was pushed abruptly away, he backed off and whined, unable to understand why one of his precious boys would order him away. Hub did his best to ignore the confused look on Pal's face.

"Go on, boy! Please!" Hub begged the dog as smothered giggles filled the room behind him.

At last Pal began to understand that no one was coming out to play. He'd have to make his own fun. Still whining at the injustice, Pal backed away, all the while looking round at Hub in brown-eyed appeal in case there had been some mistake.

Feeling like a traitor, Hub pulled his head back inside the window and shut it before Pal changed his mind and tried again. But Pal, tail drooping, padded around the corner of the school and disappeared from sight.

As Hub returned to his seat, Max took back control. "All right class, the excitement's over. I'd like to start this morning with penmanship."

Max wrote the word "penmanship" on the board in the beautifully rounded letters he would expect his pupils to emulate. But the other kids weren't interested in fancy lettering. Instead, they whispered, "Nice dog, Hub," sneering all the while. Hub just squared his shoulders, cocked his head and stared back. If he didn't establish a reputation for toughness right then and there, the rest of his school year was sure to be miserable.

CHAPTER SIX

For both Hub and Fat, that first day of school seemed like the longest of their lives. They couldn't wait to get out of there, and when classes were finally let out for the day, Fat clattered down the front steps with a stream of other kids and looked around for his brother. He finally spotted him leaning against the school fence, talking to some other boys. After a whole day with strangers, Fat thought he'd never been so happy to see his brother in his whole life.

"Hey, Hub!" Fat called out, hurrying over. "Where've you been? I've been looking all over for you."

Hub, who was affecting the lounging stance of the other boys, just looked at his younger brother silently. Fat found himself a little unnerved by the even more aggressive stares of Hub's new friends. The boys were kind of rough looking, Fat realized, with large boots and hair that could certainly have done with a Bailey trim. Furthermore, they had a way of standing that challenged anyone to mess with them.

"We gotta get home," Fat tried again.

Hub shrugged one shoulder and made no move to leave the other boys. He was imitating their attitudes. "I'm gonna shoot pool," he announced breezily. "You can get home by yourself, can't you?"

Fat's eyes widened at such daring. "Grandmother said to come right home ..."

The other boys looked at Hub to see whether or not he was going to run off. "Hey Hub, yer grandmother's calling!" one of them taunted.

Hub hesitated only a fraction. He wasn't going to let these New Bedford boys think he wasn't gutsy enough to do as he pleased, in spite of orders from home. He'd gotten off on the wrong foot first thing because of Pal, and he had spent noon and recess making up for it by insinuating himself with the toughest boys he could find. He lifted one shoulder in an elaborately casual shrug.

"Tell her that I stayed after school to help the teacher clean the blackboard."

Hub's new friends grinned when Fat's young face registered outright shock.

"Okay," returned Fat very doubtfully and uncomfortably. Telling a falsehood to Grandmother Bailey was no undertaking for the faint of heart.

Unable to think of anything else to say, Fat turned and trudged across the schoolyard. This was the first time he truly had been separated from his brother since they had arrived in New Bedford, and he felt it more sharply than he cared to admit. In fact, the boys Hub was with looked so intimidating that Fat wouldn't even dare, as he usually did, to tag along.

Then, just when Fat was feeling he really needed a friend, he found one. With no one to play with, Pal had been lying patiently in the grassy schoolyard all day. When he saw Fat, his ears shot up, his plumy tail waved and he raced over to meet him. Fat lit up at the sight and hurried to meet the dog.

"Have you been waiting for us all this time, Pal?"

Pal barked excitedly as if to say he certainly had. And as he jumped about Fat's legs, Pal also looked across the schoolyard questioningly at Hub. Fat followed the dog's gaze to where Hub was strolling off, scuffing his heels, with his loudly laughing companions.

"Hub's not coming. It's just me and you today, Pal," Fat said slowly, picking up a stick to throw. They played the game all the way home, with the result that Fat almost forgot about Hub until they actually rounded the corner of his grandmother's picket fence and romped into the yard.

May was sitting on the front porch doing the fine needlepoint she was so fond of when Fat came up the walk with Pal. She had settled her bulk into the big white wicker rocking chair, which matched the wicker settee in the shade behind the porch pillars. At the sight of the frisking canine, May rose up frowning. On the broad bosom of her dark dress, her customary string of pearls gleamed in the afternoon light.

"What are you doing with that dog, Henry?"

"Nothing. Pal was just walking me home from school, that's all."

"Where's your brother?"

The question had been bound to come up. Fat paused, considering his answer and hoping to get away without telling too big a whopper. "He said to go home without him."

"Oh he did, did he?" May's brows flew together and she looked as though she meant to personally set out in search of Hub that minute. Fat scrambled to head her off.

"I'm not sure ... but I think he went to wash the blackboards and then go play some pool with the boys from his class."

It was a very big mistake to mention pool to May Bailey. To her, as to a good many respectable folk, a pool hall was nothing but a smoke-filled den of vice and idleness, sure to be the ruin of any boy lured in. May dropped the needlepoint hoop onto a side table. Her eyes began to flash.

"What boys?" she demanded. "What were their names?"

Uh-oh! Fat saw an interrogation coming. He had better get away before he was blamed personally for Hub's defection. "I dunno. Why're you asking me so many questions anyway?"

"Never mind why. Go take that animal directly to Mr. Sutton's, and then I want you to come back here and tidy up your room before dinner."

"My room *is* tidy ..."

"Henry, that's enough. Go!"

There was no point in saying anything more. Fat headed for the backyard with the dog, glad to get away and hoping to play with Pal a bit before banishing him to Max Sutton's as ordered.

Unfortunately, one of Mrs. Grady's precious hens chose that moment to escape from the chicken coop. It had discovered the hole the fox had used and squeezed itself out under the close mesh of the chicken wire. Drunk with freedom, it flew up onto the picket fence and then down into the Bailey yard, just as Fat and Pal were coming around the side of the house. It was a very unfortunate judgment on the part of the hen!

Pal immediately broke away from Fat, who had been holding him by the collar, and streaked after the hapless bird, yapping madly. The hen leaped high into the air, squawking and flapping its stubby wings frantically this way and that as Pal lunged towards it.

"Pal!" shrieked Fat racing to rescue the bird. "No ... quit it!" But Pal had no intention of quitting—this was the best game of all!

The noise brought Mrs. Grady to her kitchen window. One second later, she came tearing out of her house, past the coop and into the Bailey yard, her apron flying and suds dripping from her fingers. Her chickens were very precious to her. She was horrified at the sight of a nasty dog skidding about on the grass, snapping at the tail feathers of her biggest Rhode Island Red.

"Stop it! What are you doing?" she hollered.

Fat dove and, by an incredible stroke of luck, managed to grab the chicken by the leg and snatch it away from Pal's eager jaws.

"Don't worry, Mrs. Grady. I got it, I got it!"

"Give her to me," snapped Mrs. Grady, snatching the struggling hen from Fat and tucking it firmly under her arm. Her eyes were practically bulging with indignation. She had always known that dog was up to no good, and now here was the proof. "I've got a mind to call the police and report this vicious attack!"

In those tough times, when keeping a few chickens or geese might make the difference between eating or starving, attacking any kind of livestock was a very serious crime for a dog. If a dog couldn't be trusted or controlled, then it had to be got rid of.

"Don't get your shirt in a knot, Mrs. Grady. He was only playing."

Playing! More like trying to rip the poor hen into chicken snacks was how Mrs. Grady saw it. And there was the dog still straining to get at the chicken. The woman puffed up in outrage.

"How dare you be so bold to me!"

Fat made the mistake of growing indignant in Pal's defense. "What're you gettin' so mad about for, anyway?" he hollered. "Your chicken came into our yard first."

Though this might very well have been the case, it was not, in Mrs. Grady's opinion, the place

of a defiant ten-year-old boy to say so. She glowered hotly at Fat, her eyes narrowing.

"Well, you're just about the most ill-mannered
boy I've ever met. Though I suppose it's no
wonder, with that low-class hussy of a mother
you've got. Thought she'd make a fortune when
your father died, but here you boys are living off
May Bailey's charity."

This malicious and utterly unexpected assault
took Fat completely by surprise. How dare this
woman, who couldn't even keep her chickens at
home, insult his mother? Fat gulped in a huge
breath. "Take that back, right now!" he shouted,
hurt and enraged.

All Pal knew was that Fat was suddenly very
upset. This awful woman must be attacking him.
And it was Pal's job to defend the boys he had
given all his love and loyalty to. He strained forward towards Mrs. Grady, growling at her as if
echoing Fat's words in his own expressive, doggy
way. The effect was to make Mrs. Grady even
more furious. She struck another low blow.

"Everybody in town knows the truth about the
woman."

"Liar!" shrieked Fat even louder than before.
"Take it back!"

Tears were starting up in Fat's eyes, and his

face was pale and blotchy. Mrs. Grady promptly grabbed him by the ear and twisted.

"Don't you threaten me, you little ragamuffin! Your grandmother should know better than to think she can make silk purses out of a sow's ears. Now you stay off my property."

Pal would have no one laying violent hands upon one of his boys. He began barking very fiercely. With a jerk, he broke free of Fat's grip and took off after Mrs. Grady. If Pal was terrific at chasing chickens, he was even better at chasing rude neighbors. He yapped at Mrs. Grady's heels until he had chased her right back up her own back steps and inside her house. And she was still holding onto the chicken.

Just as her screen door slammed, Fat recovered from his stunned silence and began screaming at the top of his lungs.

"Don't you *ever* say anything about my mother again or next time I'll sic my dog on you so bad there won't be nothin' left of you!"

This commotion finally brought May thumping out of the house as fast as a portly woman could move who usually walked majestically with the aid of a cane.

"Good Lord, Henry, what are you shouting about?"

"Mrs. Grady called my mother a hussy!"

Fat was now red to the roots of his hair and his chin was quivering with fury. Grasping him by the arm, May propelled him onto the porch. Pal, pleased with himself for having driven off the enemy so smartly, trotted at their heels, panting from his exertions.

"Lower your voice," May hissed warningly even as the curtains twitched at the Grady kitchen window. May had an ironclad rule that none of her family should make a spectacle of themselves in front of the neighbors.

"I won't! She said me and Hub were living off charity and—"

"That's enough," May snapped as she pointed to the door. "You go into the house!"

"She's got a big fat mouth on her," Fat flung back, too overwrought to even care what he was saying.

"You've got a pretty big one yourself. Now that's enough!"

Finally, May managed to push Fat inside, then went after Pal with a broom. Pal and his chicken chasing had been the start of it all.

"Go away, you dreadful creature! Go!"

Hearing the grimness in May's voice, Pal realized that a temporary retreat would be best. Easily, he dodged May and loped off down the lane. Shaking one beringed fist at him, May strode back inside to deal with Fat.

CHAPTER SEVEN

Hub eventually made his way back from that den of iniquity, the New Bedford pool hall. He arrived just in time to discover how much trouble he, Fat and Pal were in. When the Baileys sat around the dining table that evening, finishing their dinners, the silence was thick enough to choke on. Presiding from the head of the table, May glowered from one grandson to the other.

"The two of you ought to be horsewhipped," she seethed. "I won't stand for any more shouting at the neighbors or going to the pool hall. You have a reputation to uphold. You're a cut above the Gradys."

What May really meant was that the Baileys, as founders of the town, were expected to behave in a way that was an example to the rest of the population. Neither boy felt much like being an example for anyone. Hub and Fat exchanged hostile glances. Hub was highly exasperated that Fat had spilled the beans about the pool hall. Fat still stung from Mrs. Grady's hurtful words, and he was angry that Hub had not been there to help him. Grace, distressed by the altercation, could only toy with the carrots on her plate while the wall clock, in its carved mahogany casing, ticked with excruciating loudness behind them.

Suddenly, the strained quiet was shattered by a loud, aggressive hammering on the front door. Grace started to get up, glad of any excuse to get away from that oppressive table, but May waved to her to sit down. "That's fine, Grace. I'll get it."

Without haste, May crossed the hardwood floor to the entrance hall. The broad, paneled front door swung open to reveal Mr. Grady, who, judging by his scowl, was in a very foul mood indeed.

"There's no need to break the door down, Alastair," May told him coolly in her best leading-citizen voice.

Alastair Grady was a large, fleshy man with wavy dark hair, who turned a strange purplish color when he got stirred up. Right now, he was in no mood to defer to May's naturally imperious manner.

"Now don't get all high and mighty with me, May Bailey. I got home from work to find the wife in tears, holed up in the house on account of your grandson siccing that dog on her."

May had to back down a little. "I tried calling several times to apologize but there was never any answer."

"Apologize?" Alastair exploded. "Dot is so mad she wants me to inform the police to issue a warrant for the arrest of the boy and the dog."

At the mention of police, May stepped out onto the broad porch and shut the door behind her so that they couldn't be heard inside. A visit from the police would be very undignified indeed.

"I hardly think that's necessary. Henry's only a boy, after all, and apparently Dorothy said some very unpleasant things about his mother."

"Well, you've had a few choice things to say about her yourself, May," Alastair returned pointedly. May's distaste for Honey Bailey had been common knowledge ever since the moment Jack announced his intention to wed. The Gradys, being just next door, had seen May very much steamed up about it.

"That may be so, but I haven't said anything that I wouldn't say to her face."

This was true. One of the reasons Jack had broken off with his mother so long ago was her lack of restraint in stating her opinion of Honey.

When May Bailey thought a thing, she said it to a person's face without hesitation.

"Well, ain't that sweet of you," Alastair retorted acidly.

By now May was beginning to grow hot in the face too. She had already done her best to make up with Dorothy. Alastair Grady did not seem to know when to quit.

"Alastair, I'm not going to stand here trading insults with you. The dog is no longer on our property. I don't know what more I can do to make amends for what's happened other than apologize to Dorothy in person."

"I'll tell you what you can do. You can make sure your grandsons and that animal stay off my property."

"I could say a word or two about your chickens in my garden," May cannoned back, furious at having her goodwill thrown back in her face like that. But then, she had not seen Mrs. Grady as her husband had, quite hysterical and convinced she had escaped only by a hair's breadth from being savaged by the most vicious brute in New Bedford.

"Let me make this simple, May." Alastair Grady lumbered up one more step so that anyone with less grit than May would have been backed against the heavy door. "If I ever see those kids on my property again, I swear, I won't be responsible for what happens!"

May looked him straight in the eye with the steely glare she reserved for rebellious miners and hard-nosed bankers trying to take advantage of the silver mine. "Empty vessels make the most noise," she declared in a truly withering voice.

With a furious hiss of breath, Alastair Grady spun on his heel and stormed off home. May gave herself a moment to retrieve her composure, then hurried back inside.

The slam of the door behind May made Grace jump as she brought two plates with slices of plump apple pie to the table. Everyone looked up apprehensively as May sat grandly down. Grace set the plates in front of Hub and Fat.

"I thought we could enjoy some of this gorgeous pie for dessert," Grace offered, hoping to calm the waters and cheer up the boys.

"You put that right back where it came from!" May ordered sharply, stinging inwardly from her encounter with Alastair Grady. "I'm not rewarding these two hooligans for their misdeeds."

Grace had given up contradicting her mother many years ago. With an apologetic glance at her nephews, she picked the plates of pie up again, set them on the sideboard and sat down.

May leaned on the table, set with a good lace cloth as usual, and glared at the boys.

"You boys are not to set a foot on the Gradys' property again. Do you understand me?"

"What did *I* do ...?" Hub began. He had been nowhere near the Grady yard.

"You should have been here after school to watch over your brother instead of lollygagging around that pool hall."

Hub shot Fat another accusing look. Fat just stared down at the table, wishing he were somewhere else.

"If you boys are finished your meal," May continued, "you may as well go upstairs and go straight to bed."

At May's wave of dismissal, the boys got up and left. May, after a glance at her cold and congealed dinner, pushed her plate away with a sigh.

"This looks about as appetizing as a dirty doormat," she complained in a drained voice. "Grace, let's have that apple pie now. I could surely use something to cheer me up."

Grace could see how exhausting it was for her mother, having to deal with the consequences of bringing two energetic children into the house. The family had tried to warn her what it would be like.

"I agree with you, Mother, but you know boys will be boys, and you wanted them here."

"Well thank you for that show of support." May sighed wearily, wondering what on earth she would have done had young Violet been on her hands too. Handling Hub and Fat was taking more of a toll on her than she had bargained for.

Obediently, Grace got up and brought the pie over. She patted her mother's gray head as she set a plate down before her. The rich apple pie in its flaky crust ought to have cheered up anybody. Both Grace and her mother were excellent cooks.

Upstairs in the boys' bedroom, things were not much more pleasant. Hub and Fat sat on their respective beds with tension so thick it was almost crackling in the air. Hub was glaring at Fat, his jaw stuck out.

"Squealer!" he growled.

"Liar!" Fat fired back, determined not to be stuck with all the blame. After all, he'd come home just as Hub had told him to. It wasn't his fault if their grandmother went nuts at the mere mention of pool halls.

For answer, Hub picked up a ball of string from his bedside table, unwound a length and broke it off. Then he got up off his bed and walked to the middle of the room. Fat, thinking Hub was making straight for him with dark intentions, shrank back on the bed. Hub had been known to exercise his muscle on Fat before.

"Don't hurt me, don't hurt me!"

"Shut up or I'll positively mutilate you," Hub rasped.

Hub tied one end of the string to the heating grate and laid the rest of it out along the middle of the room, over the mat between the beds and all the way to the night table, completely separating Fat's half. Fat sat up again and watched him in some confusion.

"What're you doing?"

"I'm making a barrier." Hub turned menacingly, shaking a finger. "And if you cross over onto my side of the room, your dead carcass will be found here at dawn!"

"What if I hafta go to the bathroom or something?"

"Just pray you don't."

Hub marched back to his bed, turned his back on Fat and started reading.

Fat pulled his knees up, making himself as small as he could against the wall. Good thing he had not drunk a lot of water before coming upstairs. How great it would have been to hug Pal right about then. Fat wondered what Pal was doing and hoped he was enjoying himself, somewhere far away from all this trouble.

Chapter Eight

Saturday finally arrived, and Max Sutton at last had some time to himself. Now he could get back to tinkering with the old motorcycle. It was battered but sturdy, though even the red Indian logo on the side of the gas tank was barely visible from wear. If only Max could get it going, he would have some independent transportation he could actually afford. With a final turn of the wrench, Max hopped on the seat and gave the starter a powerful kick. The motor coughed, gurgled and fizzled out. Max got off again and stood back, scratching his head. It was going to take more work yet to get this veteran road warrior in working order again.

Nearby, Pal lay snoozing in the shade of a small maple, looking completely innocent of the mayhem he'd caused between the Baileys and the Gradys. He was, however, firmly on a leash, and the end of that leash was tied to the graying board fence that surrounded the yard.

When Hub strolled by, Pal jumped up and ran as close as the leash would allow, barking a happy greeting.

Max sighed and stopped working. When a Bailey boy showed up, it was sure to be with a problem. "Hello, Hubert. How are you doing?"

"Okay," Hub said dully. "Fat and me got kicked out of the house by Grandmother because her bridge ladies are coming this morning. Fat had to go to Uncle Bob's."

Hub still was not speaking to Fat. He hoped Doris was giving Fat a hard time over at his Uncle Bob's and Aunt Toppy's. In fact, he even hoped they were playing croquet again. Doris was Hub's and Fat's fourteen-year-old cousin. The last time they had tried to play croquet, Doris had kicked the ball into the bushes. All three of them had ended up in a free-for-all, Doris getting the better of them despite a bloody nose.

"I see," mused Max, distracted by the bike. "Hubert, look, I'm a little busy."

Hub did not move. Max wiped his hands on an oily rag and noticed the wistful looks he was casting at Pal. His eyes crinkled and he smiled as he realized what the boy really wanted.

"Say, how'd you feel about walking the dog?"

"Sure!" Hub brightened instantly at the prospect.

Max was pleased at having thought of a way to keep Hub occupied and cheer him up at the same time. "All right then. Make sure you give him a good run."

"C'mon, Pal," urged Hub, unhooking Pal's leash from the fence. "Come here."

Pal needed no persuasion. Overjoyed at being back with one of his boys, Pal leaped and cavorted all around Hub's feet before dragging him off down the lane. Smiling at the eternally right picture of boy and dog together, Max Sutton squatted down, picked up a wrench and returned to dismantling the motorcycle's clogged gas line yet again.

In the Bailey house, May and her six bridge ladies, the ones she had been playing with for years, sat around the table, the cards in readiness and eagerness to play on their faces. The group included Tootsie Miller, Marjorie Stables and Helen McCloud. As was the custom of the time, they all wore hats, even indoors, and were attired for visiting in dresses with neat collars and restrained prints. The ladies were preparing to play while May poured them coffee and Grace brought out a tray of assorted finger sandwiches and freshly baked ginger cookies. Tootsie Miller, her plumpness encased in lavender print, consulted her watch.

"Where's Dot?" Tootsie inquired innocently. "She's usually here by now."

All the others exchanged a look.

"She's not coming," said May shortly.

Tootsie waited for further explanation. "Why not?" she finally asked when May remained silent.

"Are you the last person in town to know?" exclaimed Helen with a toss of her head.

Marjorie, thin and bright-eyed, leaned forward and touched Tootsie's elbow, delighted to be the one to pass along a juicy bit of news. "May's been having a real drag 'em out fight with the Gradys."

May set down the silver coffee pot with a disapproving clunk. "Are we going to play cards or waste our time gossiping?" she demanded, determined to squelch this line of talk at once.

Which left them all with a practical problem. Tootsie brought it up.

"How will we play without Dot?"

"Well, Grace will play," May tossed off, instantly conscripting her daughter.

This, apparently, was news to Grace, and Helen glanced at her as she set down her tray. "I thought you didn't like bridge, Grace."

Grace shifted uncomfortably. In fact, she'd been avoiding bridge all her life, but she didn't see any way to escape now.

"Well, it's not that I don't like it ... exactly. I don't really know *how* to play."

All those numbers and bids and suits just turned into a jumble in Grace's head. But suddenly, this was no obstacle whatever to her mother, even though she had never before asked Grace to join in their games. May was determined that the absence of Dorothy Grady would not upset the familiar bridge routine.

"Oh, you don't need to know how to play, Grace. You just have to turn the cards over."

May patted a chair beside her so she could keep an eye on Grace. Grace sat down and smiled weakly, not even realizing how much any decent bridge player would be horrified by May's cavalier definition of the game.

If Dorothy Grady was staying indoors, well out of the reach of chicken-chasing dogs, her husband was not. He decided to weed and water the flower beds in front of his house, which had to be kept looking smart if they were to hold their own with the imposing Bailey establishment next door.

Naturally this would be the very moment

when Hub appeared along the walk with Pal. In fact, Hub was being dragged down the street by Pal towards the house which the dog had come to regard as home. Mr. Grady had just turned on the hose to give the row of white and pink petunias a drink. He straightened and glowered as the two rushed past, even though they gave his yard a wide berth. Hadn't May Bailey promised that that animal would not be on her property any more?

Hub was panting hard and sweating from the run. "Okay, Pal," he huffed, dragging the energetic dog to a halt.

Pal skidded reluctantly to a standstill, his tongue lolling out in the equivalent of a huge doggy smile. Pal would have enjoyed the exercise a lot more if he had been able to run free, but Hub had not dared to let him off the leash. The run had done wonders for Hub, too. He had totally shaken off the morning's gloominess and looked as a youngster should on a sunny Saturday morning. His hair was tousled from the breeze, his cheeks ruddy from the exercise and his eyes sparkling with pleasure.

While Hub was trying to catch his breath, he looped the end of Pal's leash over the front railing. "I gotta get a drink of water," he gasped. The run and the last heat of summer had made him very thirsty.

Hub panted up the steps and into the house, leaving the door wide open behind him. Pal tugged on the leash impatiently, whining with eagerness to follow Hub into the place that was so full of interesting things to chew, scratch and knock over.

"Stupid mutt," Mr. Grady flung in Pal's direction.

Pal perhaps didn't care for insults. He swung around as far as the leash would let him and gave voice to his own opinion of Alastair Grady by means of a half bark, half growl that clearly said there wasn't a Grady in the universe that was even a patch on one of the Bailey boys. It was open provocation, and Alastair Grady responded by picking up his hose and aiming it at Pal.

"Shut up, you miserable mongrel," Grady yelled as the water arched towards Pal and hit him full in the ribs, soaking him instantly. Pal spun first one way, then another in an attempt to dodge the stream, but the leash and collar held him fast. Mr. Grady chuckled nastily and turned the water up full blast, delighted at this revenge. The water choked Pal's throat, pounded his eyes and hit him in the backside, making him jump about with such force that the leash suddenly tore loose from the railing. Instantly, Pal streaked for the safety of the house, the wet leash snaking through the dust behind him.

Pal headed straight for the parlor, which was where the bridge table was set up. Heralded by a tremendous scratching of his nails on the hardwood, he skidded around the open French doors and darted under the table, where he plowed into the legs of the ladies, utterly disrupting the game.

Shrieks and cries went up all round as wet fur soaked dress hems and dribbled water into shoes. Cards flew and chairs scraped back as the players scrambled to save themselves.

"Oh heavens!" Grace jumped back and dropped a bridge hand she had not been able to make heads or tails of.

Clearing out the bridge players brought Pal out from under the table again. By now, he'd had a moment to recover from his fright. Maybe the water was a game after all, since it created so much jumping around by the ladies. And a game sure made a wet fellow hungry. Pal's excellent nose took a sniff and told him there was food in the room—just above his head on the sideboard.

Now Pal had been raised by Mr. Murphy totally outdoors, so he had no indoor manners at all. Food was food whenever it was within reach. And besides, it had been a long time since Max

Sutton had thought to feed him. With a small effort, Pal boosted himself on his hind legs high enough to clear the sandwich plate in a couple of ravenous gulps.

"Shoo, get down from there! Blasted dog!" cried Grace, flapping her arms far too late to save the refreshments she had so recently labored over in the kitchen.

May, shaking water from her knees, knew at once who was responsible for Pal's misdeeds. "HUBERT!" she bellowed, loud enough to carry to the kitchen and beyond.

Hub came barreling in, scrambling after Pal and trying to grasp his leash. "Pal, no!" he lamented, recognizing Pal's next intention.

Too late! Pal arched his back, lowered his head and let loose some vigorous shakes. Water flew from his thick coat all over the bridge ladies, the coffee cups, the card table, the sideboard and the rose-patterned wallpaper. May's good silk dress was now splattered to the waist. She stood with her arms held out to her sides in disgust and fury in her eye.

"Hubert, where did that blessed dog come from?"

"I'm sorry, Grandmother," Hub mumbled guiltily, afraid he was really in for it now. "I was

just trying to take him for a walk." And he hadn't
even let Pal off the leash, either.

"Well never mind that. You take him back to
Mr. Sutton at once and you come back here
directly before your name is mud!" May's voice
was tight as twisted wire.

As fast as he could, Hub dragged Pal outside
and out of her reach. Another minute of dripping
on the rug, Hub was convinced, and Pal really
would end up being sent to the farm.

Swallowing her outrage, May set about calm-
ing her guests. She was not about to have her
afternoon wrecked by a wet dog and the loss of
some sandwiches.

"Oh girls, I do apologize. Grace, go take those
sandwiches and throw them out and bring us
some new ones."

"Can't we help you clean up?" Helen offered
as May quickly stacked the dog-spattered coffee
cups and Grace scurried out to do as she was
told.

May was appalled. Guests in her house did not
swab furniture. "Certainly not. We'll dry out in a
minute, and Edna can wipe up later." Edna was
the woman who was hired to help out around the
house. "Grace will bring us some new sandwiches
and then we'll just have tea." She sat down in an

effort to get things back to normal. "I believe it's your bid, Helen."

The ladies exchanged glances. Things certainly had livened up around the Bailey house since the arrival of Jack's boys. As they tried to put their bridge hands back together, they could hardly wait to see what kind of uproar would happen next.

May finished the bridge party with an aplomb and calm that was utterly deceptive. The minute the bridge ladies had left, she set out hotly on foot to make her views known to the fellow who had been charged with keeping Pal out of trouble—and, most of all, from troubling the Baileys.

She found Max Sutton, as usual, tinkering with the ancient motorcycle. This time he had a good part of the motor spread out on the remains of an old bedsheet. So absorbed was Max in the problem of reassembling the bits that he completely failed to notice May's approach.

Max Sutton was yet another person whom May did not fully approve of. In her opinion he was far too casual and chummy with the children to be the firm kind of schoolteacher she expected. And because she had a fair bit of influence over the hiring of teachers in New Bedford, she regarded Max as a bit of a mistake. For that reason, she examined his bent figure with sharp and measuring eyes as she turned up the driveway towards him. To find him working on a motorcycle, of all things, only confirmed his eccentricity. Teachers walked, rode bicycles or drove a battered car should they, by some miracle, ever get hold of one. They did not ride motorcycles, associated in May's mind only with the wild or the disreputable.

"Good day, Mr. Sutton," announced May from directly behind him.

Max dropped the gasket in his hand, much startled. When he saw the town's leading citizen, he scrambled to his feet in a hurry.

"Hello there, Mrs. Bailey."

"I'm searching for my grandson," May informed him stiffly. "Mr. Sutton, you seem to have fallen through on your promise to keep that dog."

Max remembered just in time not to wipe a greasy hand on his shirt. "Well, hold on Mrs. Bailey. Hubert took the dog for a walk, and he was teaching the dog how to play catch in the front yard last time I looked."

May scanned the front yard pointedly and saw no Hubert. "He isn't there, Mr. Sutton. I appreciate your offering to take the dog. Perhaps you don't realize how much trouble we've had with the animal. I am relying on you to keep it away from my grandsons."

Max found this puzzling; he could only imagine that somehow Mrs. Bailey had decided that the dog was a corrupting influence on the boys. He couldn't quite make out what all the fuss was about.

"I'm sorry."

"Mr. George Murphy returns next week to collect the animal. Mr. Sutton, I didn't expect you to be so inept at restricting that animal from running into our yard."

Max was new to New Bedford and not used to the idea that Mrs. Bailey spoke her mind directly to all those around her without any sugar coating. In spite of himself, Max began to bristle at the way she was standing there lecturing him.

"Now see here, Mrs. ..." May's look quelled his outburst. He swiftly recalled his own best interests. "I'll do my best," he finished, managing to hold his tongue.

Seeing that she had carried the day, as she had fully expected to, May continued in her high-handed way. "When they return, would you please see that Hubert comes home at once. Thank you, Mr. Sutton."

Max conceded with a barely perceptible nod. Turning herself about, May rolled her eyes at the

sky and set out for home, the silver head of her
cane and her silver hair both gleaming in the sun.

Some time after May had left, Hub hurried back
down the street towards Max's yard, tossing a
baseball to Pal. Pal jumped up, missed the ball and
chased merrily after it as it rolled past him on the
grass. Pal was thoroughly dried out now, his coat
looking all the thicker and fluffier for the soaking.
As soon as they'd gained some distance from the
Bailey house, Hub had let Pal loose, and they had
been having a terrific time ever since.

"Come on boy, get it," Hub called, urging Pal
to retrieve the well-chewed ball.

Pal ranged enthusiastically back and forth until
he found it and brought it back. Then he danced
back and forth in anticipation of the next throw in
yet one more wonderful game busy, boring Mr.
Murphy had never thought of.

Max stepped out of the yard and stopped Hub.
"Hubert, your grandmother is fit to be tied. She's
waiting for you at home, so you'd better hightail it."

"Oh ..." Hub's eyes opened in sudden apprehension. There was certain to be trouble about the
wet bridge ladies. And ... what if Pal were going to
be sent to the farm after all?

Max clipped Pal's leash on when the animal

skipped close enough and held on firmly against his protesting tugs.

"I'll hang onto Pal so he doesn't follow you." When Hub hesitated, Max gave him what he hoped was an encouragingly humorous wave. "Well, hurry home, boy, if you value your freedom." Max just had to feel sorry for a newly fatherless lad who now had May Bailey running his life.

"Okay," Hub said, but he still didn't move.

"Go ... go!" Max urged. May Bailey was not a person to keep waiting.

Hub sank to his knees and flung his arms around Pal's neck, giving him several vigorous pats. That they were the best of friends didn't matter. May Bailey had given the order and they had to part. Who knew when they would get to see each other again?

"Bye, Pal. See you, Mr. Sutton."

Hub trudged off down the street leaving Pal barking and straining at the leash towards the boy he wanted to be with more than anything in the world. Only when Hub was totally out of sight did Pal sit down in defeat. And long after Max had tied Pal to the fence and returned to working on the motorcycle, Pal remained gazing yearningly in the direction Hub had gone.

CHAPTER NINE

When Hub walked into the kitchen, he found Fat already seated at the table. He looked as though he had not had the best of times at his Uncle Bob's house, and apprehension was creeping across his face.

"Hubert, come and sit down. I want to talk to you boys."

May had on her disciplinarian face and she was holding herself with military straightness. It was clear that someone was about to get a dressing down. Hub slumped into a chair, his arms crossed defiantly. His grandmother stood against the spotless white wainscoting and looked disapprovingly from one to the other.

"The Gradys and I have been neighbors for twenty-five years. We never spoke one harsh word to one another until you two came on the scene."

May was conveniently forgetting a number of tiffs in the early years, when Jack and Bob used to get into boyhood scrapes involving the neighbors' property. May's intimidating manner had kept the Gradys quiet back then, but they had not forgotten all the times they had to bite their tongues. In recent years, the Gradys had grown too used to peace and quiet. The sudden arrival of two boys and a dog had completely upset the delicate relations between the parties, and now May had to do something to restore them.

"They started it!" Fat jumped in, determined not to take the brunt of this attack. He hadn't yet heard about Pal's more recent offenses at the bridge party.

"I don't care who started it." May grimaced. "They've shown their true colors, that's for sure. But I intend to put an end to it. Tomorrow evening I am going to a meeting of the I.O.D.E., the Imperial Order of the Daughters of the Empire. And you are going to come with me, young man, and apologize to Mrs. Grady."

Fat's mouth popped open almost wide enough to show his tonsils. The very idea of a public apology made him twist in his chair. Besides, it was unfair. "But she's the one that said everything. Why should I have to apologize?"

"I'm sure if you say you're sorry, Henry, she will too," May answered him. But Fat didn't buy the argument—the blow it would be to his personal dignity was too high a price to pay.

"Why should I be sorry?"

May was not used to being contradicted. One eyebrow went up and she shook her double chin. "You have two choices, young man. You can either do as I have asked you to do and apologize, or you can go upstairs and stay in your room until you change your mind. Believe me, one way or the other, you will tell Mrs. Grady that you are sorry."

Fat made his choice instantly. Pushing back his chair, he marched down the hall and up the stairs. The next moment the whole house echoed to the slamming of the bedroom door. May twitched imperceptibly at the sound and frowned all the harder.

"Can I go now?" Hub asked, hoping to extricate himself quietly from the whole fiasco.

"Yes, Hubert." May sat down heavily. "Oh, Lord give me strength ..."

Hub made his escape as quickly as he could. Apologizing publicly was a horrible punishment, and Hub could not help but be in sympathy with his younger brother. He retreated to his favorite spot in the backyard and sat down under a maple tree to think about the matter.

Later that evening, Grace brought up a dinner tray to an unrepentant Fat. She found him sitting on his bed with his arms around his shins and his chin resting on his knees. He was the very picture of stubborn determination.

"Your grandmother fixed you something to eat, Henry."

"Tell her to keep it. I'm not hungry," Fat answered obstinately. For Fat to refuse good food was ominous indeed. After all, he'd got his nickname not so much for the inches around his waist as for his unquenchable appetite. Yet, with his mother's honor at stake, he had made up his mind to stay in his room till he was a gray old man, if need be, or maybe starve to death in the process.

Grace set the wicker tray down on the bedside table and sat down on the bed next to Fat. For a silent moment, she searched for the right words. Grace, after all, had had a lot of experience dealing with May.

"Maybe you should just do as she asks, Henry." She ignored Fat's mulish look. "You know how proud and stubborn she is. She doesn't give in easily, especially if she feels strongly about something. You're a lot like her in that respect."

Fat was not at all flattered by the comparison. "I don't see what I did that was so bad," he grumbled. "I've seen Grandmother gossiping with Mrs. Grady over the fence plenty of times. Maybe she's the one that started saying all that rotten stuff about my mom in the first place."

Grace was shocked that Fat could think such a thing. She hurried to put him straight. "No, no, sweetie-pie. She might not get along with your mother, but she would never say something like that about her in public. She's a family member."

"She sure doesn't treat Mom like a family member," Fat complained, remembering all too vividly his mother having to leave them behind because she wasn't invited to stay on in the roomy Bailey house.

"Well, your grandmother's harder on family than she is on other people. But loyalty and family pride are more important to her than anything else." Grace squeezed Fat's hand and said more softly, "She'll soften towards your mom in time, Henry. I really believe that."

Grace stated this with such kindness and conviction that Fat found himself latching onto this fresh shred of hope in spite of all his resolution to the contrary. He missed his mother so much. He would do anything for them to be together again.

"Do you think Grandmother might hurry it up some and let my mom move back if I went over there and said I was sorry?" If this was a way of getting her back, the sacrifice of his own pride was a small price to pay for it.

Grace gazed for a moment at the sepia- toned pictures on the walls—pictures of her brothers Jack and Bob when they were boys. The room used to belong to them when they were young. Boyhood reminders of handsome, laughing Jack Bailey were everywhere, including model airplanes Jack had built and a shelf of well-thumbed books about adventure. Fat looked very much like his father had at his age. Because of the feud over Honey, Grace had missed a good many years of being able to see her brother and watch his family grow. Jack's death had been a real tragedy for her. Now, like Fat, she only wanted the battles to end.

"I don't know, but it certainly couldn't hurt."

"Lemme think about it," said Fat, with the air of a diplomat with a very knotty decision to consider.

"Okay."

Leaving the tray behind, Grace got up to return to the dining room. Fat merely glanced at the food before leaning back to stare up at the plaster ceiling, thinking hard.

Down in the dining room, May, Grace and Hub sat eating their dinner in silence. Hub finished his food and glanced uncomfortably at Fat's empty chair. Then he pushed his empty plate away. He could not help but think that Fat must be famishing upstairs.

"Do you wish to be excused, Hubert?" May asked.

"I was thinking maybe I should go up and check if he's all right."

"Oh yes. By all means."

Hub put down his napkin, shoved himself back from the dining table and slipped upstairs. He was worried about Fat and sorry now that he had let him go home from school alone. If they'd been together, surely Pal wouldn't have gotten them into all this trouble. The pool hall, with its grubby floors and down-and-outers lounging around, had been a disappointment. Hub hadn't liked it one bit, though he certainly wasn't going to admit this out loud to the fellows he had gone with. Next time, though, he'd have more sense than to let himself get lured into such a place.

When he pushed open the bedroom door, Hub found Fat lying on his bed staring upward, his normally easygoing face tight with a swirl of thoughts. He was still thinking very hard about the apology. As the door opened, Fat quickly turned his back to face the wall. Hub stood looking at him for a long moment before he spoke. Stubbornness and suppressed misery were evident in every line of Fat's young body.

"You can't stay up here for the rest of your life, Fat."

Fat could not forget how angry Hub had been with him for telling about the pool hall. His jaw tightened. "I thought you weren't talking to me."

The string dividing the room seemed just plain silly now. The heat of Hub's anger was long past. He and Fat should be sticking together, not scrapping. Suddenly, Hub felt protective of his younger brother and wanted to help.

"Look, why don't you just say you're sorry and get it over with?"

Fat rolled over, stuck a hand behind his head and eyed his brother beadily. A hard little knot sat stubbornly inside his chest as he admitted what had been troubling him all afternoon. "How can I say I'm sorry when I'm not? That's lying."

"It's not lying. It's being polite."

This line of reasoning caused Fat to look quite confused. To clarify the matter, Hub scooped up a forkful of orange mush from Fat's dinner tray.

"When Aunt Grace asks you how you like your mashed turnips, you say, 'Fine, thank you.' The truth is you don't really like them at all. You're saying that to be polite to her. Well, it's the same thing apologizing to Mrs. Grady."

Fat considered the congealed vegetables for a long moment and finally began to grasp the idea. However, he stuck at the particulars. In his mind blossomed a picture of the entire female population of New Bedford facing him in rows and rows. And, of course, he would be standing there with his tongue so tied up it might not move again for a week.

"But Grandmother's making me go up in front of a buncha ladies at her stupid meeting. What am I going to say?"

Hub came closer, scuffing the string on the floor out of the way with his toe. He'd have no more of a childish thing like that now that Fat was really in trouble. Bailey boys helped each other when threatened from the outside. "I'll help you practice if you want."

This generous offer caused Fat to sit up on the bed and look at his brother with grateful eyes. Fat had always been a tagalong, trying to get Hub to like him and let him in on things. Now it actually seemed to be happening.

"Okay," he agreed cautiously.

Down in the kitchen, not much later, May and Grace were inspecting one of the potted begonias May was so fond of raising.

"I think you've done a wonderful job," Grace was saying as she poked the soil with her finger. "Look how much it's improved. It's green, it's full. Lovely. Although the dirt seems dry. What do you think?"

Absorbed in plant care, they did not see Fat right away when he padded quietly down the stairs, followed by his brother. Fat edged closer, nudged on by Hub. Without Hub to help him, Fat might chicken out and run back upstairs again.

"I'll do it, Grandmother," Fat piped up, causing May to swing round, startled. Grace almost dropped the plant, which was in one of May's heavy china jardinieres. Satisfaction began to fill May's face as she realized what Fat was talking about. She granted him a regal tip of her head. "Good. Thank you, my boy."

Hub poked Fat again. Fat found it within himself to offer further politeness. "You're welcome."

After Hub and Fat had made their escape, May shot a faintly triumphant smile at Grace, certain it had been her own forceful discipline that had brought about the change. She was, after all, accustomed to being right.

"There, you see? That wasn't so difficult was it, Grace? Now excuse me."

As May moved by Grace and turned her back, Grace chuckled to herself and rolled her eyes at the begonia. Privately, she believed it was the little talk she and Fat had had previously that had changed the boy's mind. She congratulated herself on her own powers of persuasion.

Calling an end to the feud had revived Fat's appetite. Back up in his room, he ate what he could of his cold dinner, carefully avoiding the mashed turnips.

Hub examined the shelf of books that had once belonged to his father. Hub, who loved to read, had already been through them all. After some thought, he selected a crumbling volume of *The Boy's Own Annual* and brought it over. *The Boy's Own Annual* was a thick hardcover book of exciting tales, poems, puzzles and facts that came out every year for the entertainment of boys lucky enough to get one. This one had a dark-brown cover with a picture of a boy hiking up a mountain trail on the front. The boy was accompanied by a cavorting dog who looked quite a lot like Pal. Some of its pages were loose and bits of the binding flaked off the spine.

"Grandmother said to be really careful with that," Fat warned. "It's really old."

"Everything in this house is really old, including her."

They almost grinned at each other. Hub flipped through the annual until he lit upon a page that looked promising.

"Here's something good. You could recite this poem." Hub knew that Fat couldn't be left to think up something on his own or the apology would be dreadful. With a poem to follow, he couldn't go off the track that badly.

Fat peered over at it, frowning. He didn't know very much about poems and promptly forgot any he was forced to learn in school. "Are you sure?"

"Sure I'm sure. It's exactly the kind of goody-goody thing all those old biddies will like." Hub handed his brother the book. "Start memorizing."

Hub was no great shakes at judging poetry either. He had picked the first poem he came to that looked about the right length to memorize and wasn't about dogs. The poem was called "Don't Read Trash," with the title in large, bold letters as if to drive the point home.

Fat began reading haltingly, with distaste. "'Don't Read Trash. Should you ask me, Are there pleasures for us all beneath the sun?'" He stopped and looked up, making a face at the stilted words. "Do I have to?"

"Yes! Keep reading."

Setting his teeth, determined to do whatever he had to, if only in the best interests of his mother, Fat bent his head and began again, making his way through each word laboriously. The exercise brought up all kinds of jittery memories of reading in front of the class at school.

"'I should answer, There are treasures in the reach of everyone' ..."

CHAPTER TEN

After a great deal of work, and a great deal of coaching from Hub, Fat finally got the poem etched into his mind. None of this helped his apprehension as the evening of his apology approached. Over and over in his mind, he saw himself squirming and sweating while all the women of New Bedford watched.

At dusk, cars lined the streets in front of the town hall where a sign reading "Meeting Tonight" proclaimed that the ladies were gathering in force. The Bailey car drew majestically up by the curb.

May, Grace, Hub and Fat got out. Both boys were squeezed into their best clothes and slicked up to within an inch of their lives. Fat was still practicing under his breath, as he had been practicing, in increasing dread, all day.

"Ladies of the Local Chapter," he recited in a monotone. "I stand before you today to show Mrs. Grady that I am serious about ... my intentions ... about something ..."

"Hey, try to sound a bit more enthusiastic, okay?" Hub said as Fat began to drag his feet. Fat had begun to look very much like a boy wondering why he was marching voluntarily to his own execution.

The town hall, handsome and conservative, like so many of New Bedford's institutions, had been built in better times with money from the silver mine. The ladies at the meeting filled a good part of it, sitting on wooden chairs that had been set out in rows just as Fat had first imagined. Fortunately for him, there were a number of preliminaries that had to be got through to get the meeting truly underway.

While the meeting was formally opened and pressing business voted on and dispatched, Hub and Fat waited in the hallway outside the meeting room. Fat, growing more restless by the minute, continued to mutter poetry under his breath, while Hub kept peeping in to try and keep track of the proceedings.

Finally, the meeting progressed to the portion set aside for uplifting entertainment. Hub and Fat edged closer to the door to watch as Toppy Bailey and their cousin, Doris, recited a poem to the I.O.D.E., complete with florid gestures and swooning looks. Doris had, without doubt, been coached by her mother, who had once been a pillar of the New Bedford Dramatic Club.

"'Thou art weak who all upholdest,'" Doris intoned in a somewhat nasal voice. "'Thou art bound who settest free; Thou art small who all infoldest, Thou art born, Eternity.'"

Hub and Fat craned their necks to see Toppy, with her hands folded in front of her and what passed for a transported expression on her face.

"'O what wonders thou art doing, Jesus,'" Toppy declaimed, rounding each syllable resonantly as she spoke, "'for the sons of men, Eden's lost in love pursuing, Till Thou woo them home again!'"

The audience sat still as mice in their seats, fascinated by Toppy's ringing delivery. Besides, Toppy was a Bailey, and no one wanted to be impolite.

"See what I told you, Fat?" Hub whispered encouragingly. "They eat this poetry stuff up. Do it exactly like Aunt Toppy."

The ladies all looked quite enthralled, except for Dorothy Grady, who was gossiping with Marjorie Stables, most likely getting the lowdown on what had happened at May's last bridge meeting—the one she very pointedly hadn't attended. Fat glanced worriedly at her, afraid that she, of all the people there, might prove utterly impervious to poetry. When the recitation was finished, a gratifying round of applause followed. Toppy and Doris looked pleased with their own performance. Bowing and smiling, they made their way from the platform down to their chairs.

May Bailey rose to her feet, looking quite grand in her navy felt hat with the feathers and suit to match. "Our thanks to Mrs. Robert Bailey and her daughter, Doris, for a profound rendition. And now," May beamed, "I'm very pleased to present my grandson, Henry Bailey."

In sheer fright, Fat gulped hard and looked as though he might actually run out the door and down the street. Hub blocked his escape and pushed him into the meeting room before he could bolt. May came to meet him and ushered him up the front amidst more polite applause. Before he knew it, Fat found himself all alone on the podium facing the ladies. Even May had taken her seat in the first row and was looking at him, just like all the others, expectantly.

Panic struck at Fat. All he saw were rows and rows of hats—feathered hats, felt hats, sateen hats, beaded hats, netted hats. And underneath each hat a pair of eyes fixed on him with intense curiosity, showing that they had all heard, by now, of his run-in with Mrs. Grady. Fat looked frantically around for Hub and spotted him taking a chair as near as he could to the front. The place was so quiet that Fat thought for sure they could all hear his heart thumping crazily against his ribs. There was nothing for it but to screw up his courage and begin to speak.

"Ladies of the Local Chapter, I want to ... to snow Mrs. Grady ..."

Fat faltered as a flurry of titters greeted his mistake. He was horrified to discover that his voice had been squeaking. His eyes flicked to Doris, who was sure to be judging him by the standard of her own excellent performance. Doris considered herself superior to her rough-around-the-edges cousins from North Bridge.

"Uh ... what I meant was I want to show Mrs. Grady that my intentions to ... um ... I want to ..."

Mired in his own confusion, Fat halted again. In another moment he was going to lose it completely, just as he had been afraid he would.

"Apologize!" Hub whispered loudly, trying to prompt him.

"Apologize ... for all the terrible things I said to her ..." Fat stumbled again, then soldiered on despite more titters. "And I want to dedicate the following poem to her ... which is entitled 'Don't Read Trash.'"

The feathers on May's hat quivered as if she couldn't believe what she was hearing. Grace covered her mouth in a combination of dismay and laughter. Mrs. Grady sat stone-faced and rigid, suspicion written all over her about what this whippersnapper of a Bailey boy was up to now. Oblivious, Fat sucked in a deep breath and launched into the work.

"'Don't Read Trash,' from *The Boy's Own Annual*." He gulped down more air as if it would keep him from passing out. "'Should you ask me, Are there pleasures' ..."

For all his effort, Fat's voice was barely audible, and his delivery was so stiff and wooden that he might as well have been a puppet trying to speak. Hub knew it would turn out to be a disaster unless he did something quick. Glancing sideways, he

began to make some rapid, surreptitious move-
ments with his hands, signaling that Fat should try
to get some more drama out of the performance by
means of some interesting gestures. Grasping the
hint at last, Fat began to imitate the soulful flutters
Doris had been making with her fingers. Without
realizing it, he exaggerated them to a hilarious
degree.

"... 'for us all beneath the sun? I should answer,
There are treasures ... in the reach of everyone!'"

Fat mimed scooping up a huge armful of trea-
sure, staggering slightly backward, to indicate the
size of the load. Despite Fat's earnestness, grins
began to appear, followed by titters and hastily
smothered sputters of laughter. When laughter
began to break out in gusts, Fat realized that the
crowd was laughing at him. Or maybe—a wild
hope gripped his mind—with him?

May was now the one who was as rigid as a
post, the only sign of her embarrassment being the
tight quiver of her chin.

Far from being mortified, Fat found the laughter much preferable to the rows of staring eyes and
the concentrated silence that had greeted him
when he had first stepped up. Besides, if the ladies
were laughing, it meant they were enjoying themselves. Fat was more of a hit being funny. He

tasted the power of being able to make people laugh. Like many a budding comic before him, Fat decided to go with a good thing when it fell into his lap.

Rapidly, he became bolder and bolder in his silliness. His performance became more and more absurd as he got carried away with the effect he was having.

"'Inheritance of ages, Standard books and journals too,'" he continued, his young voice now carrying easily to the far corners of the meeting room, "'Which contain within their pages ... messages for me and you.'" He emphasized this with a large, meaningful wink. "'There are treasures, gems of beauty, Heirlooms of special worth, For they speak of Truth and Duty'..." Fat dropped to one knee and clapped a hand over his heart, "'And the things of higher earth.'"

Hub, who felt responsible for the transformation that had happened before his very eyes, was cringing and covering his face. He had created a monster! When was Fat ever going to get to the end of that poem and mercifully stop?

Fat had no intention of stopping. He began to march back and forth across the platform, talking faster and faster, arms sweeping and every bit of him now playing for laughs.

"'Good for boys of every nation, For their aim is true and high. Good for boys of every station, Bright yet some may call them dry.'" Fat pulled a sour face to emphasize the word "dry." "'These prefer, perhaps the senseless Penny Horrible and find, those are stale which aim at filling with true hope and youthful mind.'"

The Penny Horrible was a cheap, sensational novel those of refined taste thought dreadful and those with a penny to spend devoured with delight. Fat swung round on his heel and swelled to bursting in a fit of rhetoric. To look at him, anybody would have thought that Penny Horrible novels were about to rain down from the sky and rot out the brains of all New Bedford.

"'Boys!'" Fat shouted so loudly that Mrs. Grady jumped in her seat, "'You never will regret it,'" he waved his finger at the audience, "'if you act on my advice ... Read what's good, and don't forget it!'" He smiled hugely. "'Never read trash at any price.'"

Finishing up with an enormous flourish, Fat bowed to much laughter and thundering applause. The only people who didn't know what to make of him were his own family. Drunk with this triumph, he dropped to one knee and appealed melodramatically to Mrs. Grady.

"Mrs. Grady, I never meant to call you a liar, and I never meant for Pal to attack your darn chickens."

The applause died away. All eyes turned to Mrs. Grady, who looked quite petrified in her seat. Such an apology was about the last thing she had been expecting.

"Oh, go on, Dot," Marjorie Stables prompted, "forgive him. Do!"

"Yes," the other ladies chimed in when Dorothy didn't move. "He's absolutely adorable. What a charmer!"

Mrs. Grady couldn't very well do otherwise, with everyone looking at her like that. She had to bow, however reluctantly, to public pressure.

"Thank you, Henry," she conceded at last, with a little nod that surely put a crick in her neck. "I forgive you."

Fat kissed her hand with a smack that would have done credit to a Knight of the Round Table. Everyone applauded, even though Dorothy Grady removed her hand from Fat's grip as soon as she could.

Grace and Hub joined in enthusiastically. Grace had secret fantasies of being an actress herself, while Hub was just astonished by his brother's success.

Now that the meeting was over, the ladies got up from their seats and began to fuss over Fat. As had many a thespian before him, Fat sopped up the attention, infected forever with a fever for the stage.

"You must have Henry come back and speak again at our next County General Meeting in Hillsdale, May," Helen McCloud gushed, not even noticing May's continuing discomfort.

"We'll see," answered May, a not-on-your-life expression on her face.

Eventually, the crowd broke up and the people set out for home. Grace, who was driving, pulled the Bailey car into the drive in front of their house at just about the same time as the Gradys arrived home in their car. May exchanged a polite wave with them, nudging Fat and Hub to do the same. A truce seemed to be in the making. Perhaps Dorothy would even show up at May's next bridge meeting. Keeping a smile on her face for the Gradys' benefit, May climbed ponderously out of the car after her grandsons.

Instead of going into the house, May paused. "Take a walk with me in the garden, boys," she said, steering them both towards the grassy expanse bordered by May's prized spirea and forsythia bushes. The night air was warm and, in that early September, there were no mosquitoes, only some fireflies winking in the dimness. As the grass rustled under their feet, May got to what was on her mind.

"I think we should have a chat about the pitfalls of overdoing things," she told them with asperity. "You got away with it tonight. Next time you might not lead such a charmed life."

"Mrs. Grady forgave Fat, though," Hub hurried to put in. That, after all, had been the whole purpose of the exercise. It would be an awful shame to lose the benefit of it now.

"But he really wasn't sorry, were you, Henry?"

Fat shook his head. He had no intention of pretending otherwise. "I couldn't be. I love my mother and I don't think anybody should insult her."

The conviction and sincerity in Fat's voice caused May to really look at her grandson. Loyalty to Honey radiated from every fiber of the boy.

"It's quite one thing to try to defend your mother's good name, Henry, but you must try in the future to rise above other people's insults, be bigger than they are, if you are going to be a success in life."

These were wise words. And May said them with an eye to avoiding future complications like the one they had just struggled through. Thank goodness that troublemaking ruffian of a dog would be gone in a few more days.

Fat was still floating from his heady triumph in the meeting hall. Never had he imagined it could be so thrilling to stand up before a crowd and make them laugh. It had been such an altogether dizzying experience that he began to get stars in his eyes. He wanted to do it all again.

"Maybe I could be a success on stage talking to people—like tonight?"

May was unable to help relenting at the sight of ambition in her grandson. "Anything's possible," she said.

The opening was too much to miss for a boy with an aching heart and a single overwhelming desire.

"Even our mom coming to live with us again?" Hub tried cautiously.

May was silent for a long moment. Even she could not fail to be moved by the pleading look on the boy's face. "Someday ..." May finally replied, very reserved.

It was another tiny crack in the solid wall of resistance May always put up when it came to Honey.

Fat slipped his hand into May's and gave it a squeeze. It had been a very long time since any growing lad had voluntarily taken May's hand. Her head bent and the corners of her mouth curved up involuntarily. Who knew what she might have promised had they not been interrupted all of a sudden by Pal, who came bounding across the grass, his leash dragging behind him. He had managed to escape from Max Sutton's yard once again. With a cry of surprise, Fat suddenly dropped May's hand and ran over to see his canine friend. Panting and grinning, Pal jumped all over Fat, licking his face and getting dust and hair all over Fat's good suit.

"Hi Pal ... how ya doing?" Fat chortled in delight, hugging the dog and burying his face in Pal's neck.

May did not take kindly to being rejected in favor of a dog. Instantly, she reverted to her usual pepperiness.

"Don't roughhouse with that dog in your good clothes, Henry. Go in and change." And when Fat didn't seem to hear, she had to raise her voice. "That's enough, Henry."

Pal then bounded over to Hub and began jumping up on him happily, very pleased with himself that he had figured out how to get back to his boys yet once again.

"Can't he stay for just a little while?" Hub begged, longing to romp with his friend. Hub was even happier to see Pal than Fat was. He had been secretly and sadly counting off the days until Pal would be taken away by Mr. Murphy, the mine supervisor.

"No. The truce with the Gradys isn't going to last long with that dog hanging around."

"Pal won't get in their yard. I'll watch him," Hub vowed fervently, ready to promise anything just to keep Pal nearby.

May certainly wasn't going to take a chance on that. Not after all the times Pal had made a nuisance of himself already. "I said no. I don't want that dog coming over here any more." May moved between the boys and the eager dog to drop the biggest bombshell. "And I don't want you boys going over to Mr. Sutton's yard any more either."

"Why not?" Fat asked, shocked.

"Because that dog's nothing but trouble, that's why."

"Oh Grandmother ..." both boys chorused plaintively.

May grabbed up Pal's leash herself. She had learned that, with Pal, the only way to make sure he was out of mischief was to return him to his place of incarceration herself.

"There's no use trying that on for size. I've made up my mind. I'll see to this myself. Come along, Pal."

Looking back over his shoulder the whole time, Pal was half marched, half dragged over to Max Sutton's back yard, where he was securely tied up under May's watchful eye. As May stepped away, Pal gave a pitiful, protesting whine. He longed to be with the boys as much as they longed to be with him. Why did he always end up tied to the fence in this strange, cramped yard?

"I trust that's tied tightly, Mr. Sutton," May rapped out pointedly. "I'm holding you responsible. We don't want any more trouble with the Gradys."

While May was seeing to Pal's imprisonment, the boys were up in their bedroom trying to grapple with their grandmother's prohibition. They had climbed into their beds. Fat lay with his arm around his pillow staring disconsolately out the window. Clouds had rolled in, and now he couldn't even see any stars.

"I did everything she wanted," Fat muttered slowly. "It's not fair that she won't let us see Pal any more."

There were a great many things in the world that were not fair, as the boys were beginning to discover. Hub understood this a bit more than Fat, but it did not make the knowledge easy to swallow.

He rolled over and looked at his younger brother across the space between the beds.

"Well that's just the way it is. You'll have to get used to it. Now go to sleep."

There seemed no answer at all to that. With a sigh dragged from deep in his heart, Fat turned his back and pulled the covers up over his head, as if trying his youthful best to block out all the problems that continually pursued him.

CHAPTER ELEVEN

The next morning, in the Bailey kitchen, Grace was making school lunches while May set bowls of porridge down before Hub and Fat—a nourishing, rib-sticking breakfast worthy of a growing Bailey boy. Fat, refusing to meet her gaze, ignored her studiously. Hub sat down heavily in one of the wooden kitchen chairs. Both of them were thinking about Pal and wishing hard that they could see him.

Breakfast was rudely interrupted by a very sharp rap on the back door, which May opened to reveal Alastair Grady. Alastair was standing on the back stoop in his raincoat, dripping with rain and looking like a big black cloud.

"Good morning, Alastair." May greeted him with careful pleasantness. This was the first test of their newly restored neighborliness.

Alastair Grady cast her a glare that was anything but neighborly. His face was the color of old bricks and he bristled with anger as he hit them with his thunderbolt.

"I'm not here to socialize, May. That dog went after our chickens again last night. Killed two of them this time."

Both boys dropped their porridge spoons in shock. May regarded Alastair Grady calmly. "The last time I saw that dog he was tied up in Mr. Sutton's yard. Are you sure a fox hasn't killed your chickens?"

Mr. Grady was more than sure—at least in his own mind. "I am sure," he ground out in a voice heavy with meaning. "Now something has to be done about this, May." Chicken-killing was a crime for which a dog would have to pay with his life—and Alastair Grady clearly wanted payment in full.

May remained unmoved by Mr. Grady's bluster. As far as May was concerned, she had done her best about Pal and didn't want to deal with dog problems any more. There, at the door, she washed her hands of the whole thing.

"Well, it's really no affair of mine, Alastair. The dog's owner will be back next week. Meanwhile, the dog is at Max Sutton's. You should take it up with him."

"Oh, I'll take it up with him all right. You can count on it!"

Alastair Grady turned abruptly and tramped away towards his own yard. May closed the door and firmly changed the subject. She didn't want to hear another word about that dog.

"Grace, it's raining. You should drive the boys to school, it would be better."

Fat pushed his chair back and jumped up, outraged that Pal had been accused of this terrible crime and frightened about the consequences.

"Pal didn't kill any chickens."

"I don't want to hear any more about it," May snapped. "Now finish your breakfast before you're late for school."

But even at school there was no escape from the turmoil over Pal. Mrs. Grady, even more indignant than her husband, had taken action. She had steamed all the way down to the school in time to corner Max Sutton in the hall before classes began. Hub and Fat, trailing a group of other kids, spotted her and instantly flattened themselves against the wall just around the corner to listen.

"Mrs. Grady," Max was saying in his best schoolteacher manner, "I know you've had problems with Pal before, but I don't think he was responsible this time. I had him tied up in the yard all night."

Mrs. Grady was not convinced. After all, escaping yards was Pal's specialty. Hadn't she seen the Baileys time after time chasing after that animal and dragging him back to be tied up again?

"Must've gotten himself loose, then," she said, giving Max a suspicious glare.

The boys edged steadily closer, still keeping themselves at a prudent distance. Their hearts were beating hard for fear of what might happen to Pal now.

"Well," returned Max, unable to resist a little playful sarcasm, "he was still tied in the yard when I got up this morning, so I'm not sure how he managed to kill your chickens and then tie himself back up on the leash. Unless he's some Great Houdini dog.

The Great Houdini was a magician famous for escaping from straitjackets, locked boxes, chains and handcuffs, even while upside down and under water.

Mrs. Grady did not take kindly to having her

opinions contradicted. In fact, she bristled all over. "You are in no position to make jokes at my expense, Mr. Sutton. I can have my husband see to it that the school board tosses you out on your backside in a second."

In those days there was no such thing as job security. A job, if one was lucky enough to have one, usually depended on the goodwill of whoever was in charge. The school board, with Mr. Grady in a leading position, was in charge of Max—and he really needed this job. He backtracked instantly in an effort to save his bacon.

"I'm sorry, Mrs. Grady. I meant no disrespect."

"Oh, I think you did, and I don't think you're one darn bit sorry." Mrs. Grady leaned forward and looked Max narrowly in the eye. "But you will be. I'll see to it."

Max watched anxiously as Mrs. Grady stormed off down the hall. Then he turned away to get to his morning class.

Fat and Hub stepped out as the angry woman huffed past them.

"Mrs. Grady," Hub called out, hoping she'd stop.

Mrs. Grady glanced back, saw who it was and kept on walking. The boys dashed after her, caught up and blocked her way. They just had to clear Pal's name.

"Mrs. Grady ... wait. Mrs. Grady, are you gonna call the police on Pal?"

"Cause if you are," Fat added desperately, "it's not right. Pal wouldn't hurt a fly. He's not like that."

Mrs. Grady drew herself up, looked down her nose icily at the two anxious boys and gave a snort. She'd already seen Pal once before going after one of her hens. Why, at the very moment Fat had been giving that ridiculous performance last night and kissing her hand and making her feel like a fool, that odious animal had no doubt been sneaking towards her chicken coop, its mouth slavering. Fat's apology was nothing but a farce.

"I have nothing to say to you boys. Now, please excuse me."

It was useless to protest further. Besides, the bell was ringing. Mrs. Grady slammed out the front door, leaving the boys to a day in school racked with worries that did very little for their concentration on arithmetic and history and utterly wrecked their spelling.

CHAPTER TWELVE

The sense of foreboding that haunted the boys all day proved to be well founded. When they pushed out of the school doors at the end of the day, they intended to rush over to Max Sutton's yard to see Pal, regardless of what their grandmother had ordered. Instead, they found their Aunt Grace waiting on the school steps for them, holding her purse very tightly in both hands.

"Boys, your grandmother asked me to bring you home."

Grace was never good at hiding anything. The distress written all over her face sent an immediate bolt of alarm through Hub and Fat.

"What, is something wrong?" Fat demanded shakily, immediately imagining the worst. "Is my mother sick?"

"No, no, it's not your mother."

In spite of schoolmates watching, Grace took them each tightly by the hand and set out for home. She didn't say any more and the boys were afraid to press her. Grace was so upset she was almost ready to start hiccuping.

When they got back to the house, Grace led them towards the yard. Before she had a chance to explain, they saw their grandmother standing over something wrapped in a blanket. As soon as May saw the boys, she walked quickly towards them, intercepting them before they could get much further.

"Now boys," Grace said quickly, resting her

hands on their shoulders and trying to prepare them, "something's happened. Pal was killed today. We found him by the drive. He seems to have been hit by a car."

Fat's mouth dropped open and Hub went pale, as though someone had just punched him hard from behind. Then the shock hit, full force.

"NO!" Hub shouted, pushing past Grace in spite of all her efforts to keep him back.

"Now Henry, there's nothing you can do for him now," May offered gently.

"Let me go," cried Fat, wriggling in Grace's grip. "I wanna see him!"

May nodded to her daughter, knowing now that there would be no keeping the boys away from the blanket-covered shape on the grass.

"Let him go."

Grace released Fat and stepped back. His knees barely holding him up, Hub ran over to the blanket, with Fat right behind him. The blanket was the gray one May kept out back to put over her knees in the evening cool when she sat on the porch. Kneeling down, Hub could not, at first, bring himself to lift it.

"How could this have happened?" Hub asked, unable to conceive of a world without Pal gamboling about in it.

"Pal ..." Fat cried, with a lump in his throat.

"You don't need to look at him, boys," May told them, walking up. Her head was bent in sympathy for the hard blow the boys were suffering.

"No." Hub's voice was breaking. "I wanna see him ..."

Fat choked up. "Pal ..." he moaned brokenly.

Fat knelt beside Hub. Ever so gently, Hub lifted up the blanket to reveal Pal, lying on his side, his leash, chewed in half this time, bunched beside him There was mud on Pal's soft brown fur from the rain. Otherwise, there were no marks to be seen. He might almost have been sleeping. Yet he was so limp, so still that there could be no question that he really was dead. The playful, lively, mischievous spirit that had been Pal was long gone from the lifeless body.

After a very long moment of gazing down, Hub covered Pal again, tucking the blanket around him tenderly. He turned to his grandmother, his face still pale from the shock.

"Do you think Mr. Murphy would mind if we buried Pal out back by the tree?" Hub asked slowly, as if he were having trouble pushing the words out.

May, who had been so impatient with Pal in life, now found that she had to struggle to maintain her composure. She began to remember what it was like to really love a faithful pet. The presence of these two lads was loosening up emotions she hadn't felt in years and years.

"No, I don't think he'd mind at all. I'll get the shovel."

Hub turned back to the familiar shape under the blanket. His shoulders heaved. "I'm gonna miss you, Pal ..."

"Pal ..." Fat whispered brokenly, beginning to realize that there would be no more romps down the lane, no more inquisitive nose thrust into his hand, no more warm body to sleep at the foot of his bed.

Hub picked Pal up in his arms, making sure the blanket was wrapped around him. Fat followed as Hub carried the bundle down to the big chestnut tree that cast its cool shade in the sunshine and sheltered from the rain. Grace trailed her mother over to the shed to get a shovel. When they had found a sturdy spade, they walked back across the yard to where the boys had picked out a spot. Neither could say a word.

As they walked through the yard, the curtains twitched at the Grady kitchen window, for Mrs. Grady missed nothing that went on in the Bailey yard. Mrs. Grady was peering out of her window as the two women passed. May stopped and shot her neighbor a withering glare which did its work. Swiftly, the woman disappeared.

Luckily for Mrs. Grady, Hub hadn't seen her. May handed him the shovel. Hub paused with his head bent, then purposefully thrust the point of the shovel into the earth. As Hub turned over the fresh sod, Grace put her arms comfortingly around Fat.

As a labor of love, Hub dug a fine, deep grave for Pal right where the chestnut branches would shade and shelter him the most. When Pal was laid to rest, Grace and May retired to the house to leave the boys alone to say goodbye to their friend.

Later on, Grace stood in the kitchen drying a dish and looking out the window. May came in, leaning on her cane.

"Is he still out there?" May inquired.

When Grace nodded, May turned and started outside again. Hub sat by Pal's grave, which was now a neatly packed mound of brown earth in the green lawn, with a stone marking the place, Pal's name painted on it in white letters. Hub's eyes were red from crying. May came slowly over and sat down beside him. Neither said a word as they listened to the rustle of the chestnut's leaves and felt the emptiness of being without Pal.

"We could move some of those blue irises from the front of the house and plant them under this tree," May offered, wanting to do something to help Hub's grief. "They come up so pretty every spring. It would be a nice tribute to Pal, wouldn't it?"

Hub nodded but did not meet her eyes, afraid he'd start to cry again. Pal, he supposed, would like irises.

"If we hurry," May continued, "we could move them before it gets dark."

Wordlessly, they both got up. May moved to take Hub's hand but he walked quickly ahead of her towards the house.

Just then, Mr. Grady stepped outside to move some trash. Hub saw him and suddenly, the huge question of whose car had killed Pal flew into his mind. The look on Alastair Grady's face only confirmed Hub's suspicions.

"You hit Pal with your car, didn't you!" Hub shrieked—so loudly and furiously that Mr. Grady backed up a few steps and almost fell into his own trash bin.

The sudden fierceness of Hub's accusation caused Mr. Grady to jab a finger in the boy's direction. "He sets a foot in my yard, I'm calling the police, May!"

Hub still had earth staining his hands from digging. Some of it was smeared across his face where he had been wiping at tears, giving him an eerie, savage look. Mr. Grady had no idea what the boy was capable of in a state like that. May managed to grasp Hub's arm and turn him around to face her. The last thing she needed was her grandson attacking their neighbor.

"Hubert, let me handle this. Hubert, please."

Hub quivered in his grandmother's grip for a moment, as if he meant to fly at Alastair Grady no matter who tried to stop him. Then sadness seemed to overwhelm him again, draining his energy.

"Wait for me by the house," May told him quietly, nodding towards the back porch.

Over the fence, Mr. Grady went back to putting out the trash, as if ignoring the Baileys would make the whole situation go away. Out of the corner of his eye, he saw Hub reluctantly go up to the back steps and stand there, his young face tense with emotion.

Alastair should have been looking in the other direction. May marched over to the Gradys' gate, let herself through and caught Mr. Grady before he could make a hasty retreat back inside the kitchen door.

"I only want to know one thing, Alastair," May asked him evenly. "Was it your car that hit the dog?"

Many a tougher man than Alastair had quailed before May Bailey. The steel in her voice penetrated to his bones. The man fell silent, with a guilty look on his face more damning than any words could possibly have been. May felt a blast of icy anger sweep through her. Sure as anything, Alastair had killed the dog and wasn't even going to bother to tell anyone about it. How rotten could you get over a couple of lost chickens!

Well, May had her ways of dealing with such a person. Part of her family had been hurt and she wasn't going to stand for it. All her formidable protectiveness welled up as she looked Alastair hard in the eye. "You know what I wish? I wish I'd told the whole town I saw you coming out of that hotel with Bonnie Martin in North Bridge last fall ..."

Alastair Grady's face turned a pasty white, then a violent, fiery red as he found himself mortified to the very roots of his hair. His glance skittered towards the kitchen window, on the awful chance that his wife might be near enough to hear.

"Now now, May," he stammered, hands flung up as if to ward off a further attack, "you're ... you're a good Christian woman."

So she had hit the mark, dead on! Unswervingly, May went in for the kill. "And I'm sure my grandson Henry would be happy to recite that tale to the fullest extent of his public-speaking talents."

Public exposure! The mere threat struck Alastair Grady speechless. His color reverted from scarlet back to a cheesy gray as he imagined the assembled residents of New Bedford scandalized by such a tale. He'd be ruined, through and through.

"All right, all right, it was an accident," Alastair burst out. "I mean, the dad-blamed dog. It just ran in front of me—out of nowhere, dragging that leash behind it.

May measured her neighbor with a gaze that would have fused metal. Alastair couldn't stand it. He was in the wrong and he knew it. His shoulders gave a heavy shrug. "Look, I'm sorry—even if the animal had no more manners than a ... a hooligan. I'll get Dorothy a couple of new hens."

The crickets chirped while May stood there deciding whether Alastair was telling the truth. At last, she decided that Pal's death had not been deliberate, despite her neighbor's animosity towards the dog. Now that she had the culprit caught out and cornered, May decided to issue a decree.

"I don't ever want to hear you or Dorothy say another word against any member of my family— including my daughter-in-law Honey. Because if you ever hurt my boys again, so help me God, I'll not be responsible for what happens!"

May began majestically making her way back to her own yard. On the way, she paused to fire one parting shot. "And Alastair," she added, "if you want to keep those new hens, I recommend you fix the wire in the coop where the fox is getting in."

Alastair had, all the while, been edging towards the back door. The instant May started walking again, he turned tail and fled inside. Satisfied, May entered her own yard again and held out her hand to her grandson.

"Let's go and get some of those irises for Pal."

Through his tears, Hub had watched in astonishment as May defended his mother and sternly forbade the Gradys from ever uttering slander against her again. Now, as the two of them began to walk around to the front of the house where May's famous blue irises grew in banks, Hub felt some kind of weight lifting off his chest. It was almost as though Pal were frisking at his heels again, pleased that his boys had found out their grandmother really was on their side after all. Hub might have just lost one friend, but he had found another. Much comforted, Hub smiled at last and slipped his hand into that of his grandmother, squeezing it tight.

WIND AT MY BACK

①

LEAVING HOME

Life will never be the same. Hub and Fat knew that the Great Depression had come to their home town—their friends and neighbors are now very poor and even food seems scarce—but they didn't think it would affect them. After all, Dad did own the local hardware store. Then the bank forecloses on Jack Bailey's loan, and everything changes—fast.

Hub and Fat suddenly find themselves plunked down in the stuffy home of their dour Grandmother Bailey—who has too many rules and not enough fun. But when real tragedy strikes, Hub and Fat realize there's more at stake than just fun.

ISBN 0-00-648149-3
$5.99
trade paperback

HarperCollins*Publishers*Ltd

WIND AT MY BACK

②

NERVES OF STEEL

It's just not fair. Hub's good at everything—
including all the sports that Fat finds impossible.
So when Max Sutton, the local schoolteacher, puts
together an athletic team to compete for the local
Fall Fair's Human Pyramid Contest, Hub naturally is right in the thick of things. Who needs a
runt like Fat around? But as the pyramid nears
completion, everyone realizes that someone Fat's
size is just what the team needs.

Now if only Hub and Fat could actually *get* to
the fair in time for the contest. With Aunt Grace
driving, you never know what's going to happen.

ISBN 0-00-648154-X
$5.99
trade paperback

■ HarperCollins*Publishers*Ltd